She turned to face him, struggling for something to say.

"Well, good night, then. The morning will be here before we know it."

One of his wry smiles teased at his mouth. "Good night, Moira." He hesitated a moment longer. Moira had the sense he was waiting for something. When it didn't come, he gave her a small bow and departed her chamber, heading to his room across the salon. Only when he was gone did she realize what he'd wanted. His name. He'd wanted her to say his name. It was a small enough courtesy to offer him after all the courtesies he'd offered her. His every thought, his every action today had been for her benefit.

Even though this wedding day must have taken an enormous emotional toll on him. He'd set all that aside for her to create the appearance of an eager bridegroom. And all he'd wanted in return was to hear his name. She would do better tomorrow, Moira vowed. She turned down the lamp beside her bed and whispered quietly into the lonely dark, "Good night, Ben."

Elizabeth Rowan lives in the Pacific Northwest, where she works as a professor. She enjoys taking long morning rambles with her dog, Bennie, and talking through her next writing project with her husband. Elizabeth plays the piano, loves to watch her three kids pursue their passions and enjoys being part of her local church.

Books by Elizabeth Rowan

Love Inspired Historical

The Major's Family Mission

Visit the Author Profile page at LoveInspired.com.

The Major's Family Mission

ELIZABETH ROWAN

LOVE INSPIRED

INSPIRATIONAL ROMANCE

LOVE INSPIRED®

INSPIRATIONAL ROMANCE

Recycling programs
for this product may
not exist in your area.

ISBN-13: 978-1-335-41893-7

The Major's Family Mission

Love Inspired
22 Adelaide St. West, 41st Floor
Toronto, Ontario M5H 4E3, Canada
www.LoveInspired.com

Printed in U.S.A.

For I am persuaded, that neither death, nor life,
nor angels, nor principalities, nor powers,
nor things present, nor things to come,
Nor height, nor depth, nor any other creature,
shall be able to separate us from the love of God.
—*Romans* 8:38–39

For Dad and Nancy, who are always
a source of support and encouragement.

Chapter One

The Blackthorne Brownstone, New York
September 21, 1846

It wasn't a question of *if* she would do something unorthodox. That was a given. It was only a question of when, which was why Moira Blackthorne approached her brother's walnut-paneled study with no small amount of trepidation on a rainy afternoon in early fall. This particular episode should not have upset him. It should not have upset anyone. It wasn't the worst thing she'd ever done, merely the latest. The worst was reserved for having stolen Robbie Farrington's clothes at the fishing hole in Saratoga when she was twelve and hardly knew better.

At the door to the study, Moira shook her skirts straight and pressed her hands against them, trying to smooth out any telltale wrinkles from sitting cross-legged in the window seat. *She* was the wronged party here, she reminded herself with a squaring of her shoulders. *She'd* been dragged home from the party—discreetly, of course, but still dragged. By rights, she should be drinking tea in Mrs. Bostwick's drawing room with all the other fine young ladies of New York City's upper crust, but Mrs. Bostwick had sent for her brother to escort her home. Mrs. Bostwick had overreacted, that was all. Everyone who knew Moira knew she was high-spirited. Nothing she did should come as a surprise to them, and dear heavens, summer had dragged on. She was bored to tears.

Moira raised her hand to knock on the door, feeling more certain of her cause. She would explain it all to Brandon. They would laugh over it together and decide Mrs. Bostwick was too prim for her own good. All would be well. Her brother loved her. She had nothing to fear from this interview.

Until she did.

From the moment she stepped foot inside the study and saw Brandon seated behind the big, polished desk that had belonged to their father, to the first words out of his mouth, "Moira, I dislike being put in this position," everything about this interview felt different. Gone was the older brother who had bought her dolls for her birthday when she was a child and had cajoled her through the difficulties of adolescence in the absence of a father *and* mother, both taken too early.

Instead, here was the shipping magnate, a man of influence and power, a man who was conscious of his family's standing in the community. In the twelve years since their father's death, Brandon had been busy preserving the family fortunes, and for the last five years that preservation had taken place during a time of economic panic. One of those efforts had resulted in his marriage. She did not know this man her brother had become, at least not very well, certainly not as well as she'd thought.

She did, however, know how to play the penitent. Moira took the seat in front of the desk, hands folded demurely in her lap. "And what position is that, dear brother?" At any moment, would he drop the mask of adult formality and burst out laughing over this latest prank. Until then, she would play along.

Today, Brandon was not fooled. "That position is being made to look like a man who cannot manage his family. How can I be trusted with larger issues like other people's money if I cannot keep one errant young woman in line?" Brandon shook his head in frustration, the mask slipping slightly. "All this time, I thought we were in this together, Moira. You and me against the world after Mother and Father died. I would protect you, raise you, and in turn, you would be a credit to *us*, to the Blackthorne family name. We were a team. These days, however, I hardly know you."

Ah, so he felt it, too. This growing apart. She'd not expected that. Guilt swamped her. Her actions had reflected poorly on her brother, his new wife and new baby boy, even on Mama and Papa in heaven. She'd thought only of herself, and even then, she'd barely thought about that. She'd been reckless. It was the only way she knew how to be anymore. There was freedom in recklessness. Freedom from grief, freedom from loss, freedom from rules. When she was reckless, she was most herself. "I am sorry, Brandon. Truly, I am." She raised penitent brown eyes, and then whispered softly, "But Edward Brant started it."

She'd gone too far. She should have quit with "I'm sorry." Brandon sighed with disappointment at the "but." "I've heard Mrs. Bostwick's interpretation of events. I might as well hear yours, too. What happened, Moira?"

This was better. Moira sat up straighter and leaned forward in earnest. "Mr. Brant claimed he was the superior shot to any in the city. I knew it to be an outright lie and you know how I can't abide a lie. I am a far better shot than he. I had no choice but to make him prove it."

She expected Brandon to nod in understanding, his expression to clear as full comprehension came to him. He knew what a spectacular shot she was. He'd taught her himself the first summer after her parents had died. Target shooting had occupied her all that summer from sunrise to sunset, something to concentrate on besides her grief, and it had been that way ever since. Brandon would understand this.

Instead his brow furrowed more deeply. "It is unseemly for a young lady of your background to challenge a gentleman in such a bold manner. To have done so in front of all the guests at Mrs. Bostwick's party was not well-thought-out."

"Fiddlesticks, Bran, who cares what is unseemly

and what is ladylike?" Moira dismissed his concerns with a wave of her hand. That was her mistake. Her brother was serious this time.

"I care, Moira, and you should care, too. I have spent the last twelve years repairing the family fortunes from the mess father left so that no one dare breathe a word of scandal about us, about you, so that you might make a good match, so that I might give you a good life along with it. You are not a young girl anymore. What might be tolerated in a girl of eighteen, first out in society, as youthful exuberance, borders on scandal in a young woman of twenty-two. You should be settled with a husband and a family of your own by now, not challenging the Edward Brants of the world to shooting contests. It's not a behavior that generally recommends a wife."

She tossed her head. "I don't want to be a wife, so we're safe there." But she didn't feel safe. Brandon, who had been her rock, was a different sort of rock today. Today, he was granite and unyielding no matter how she tried to chisel away at him. She gave a little pout, which usually worked. "You're supposed to be on my side, Bran. Since when do the Mrs. Bostwicks of the world get your favor over me?"

He pushed a hand through walnut-dark hair, thick and full like her own. "I *am* on your side, Moira. Always. But this has gone too far. The whole of New York society saw you challenge him *and* beat him. Can you imagine how that made Edward Brant feel? A man's pride is a precious, fragile thing, Moira."

He was warning her now. She could not heed it.

As if she had any consideration for Edward Brant's pride. "And yet, young men of similar background do it all the time. They sit around in billiards rooms and clubs daring each other to all nature of absurd things every day. Why, just last week Charlie Kincaid challenged Daniel Marsh to a similar shooting contest and *they* placed fifty dollars on the outcome, an outcome neither of them could guarantee. If I'd done that with *my* shooting I'd have made a fortune. I knew the outcome before the contest even started."

"Such behavior is a sin, Moira. It's hardly appropriate behavior for a girl your age who ought to know better. I can't go around cleaning up after your messes forever." Brandon's tone was firm. "So, I've decided perhaps it's time for you to go abroad for a while."

"Oh! That would be splendid!" Moira smiled, her worry falling away from her. She'd been concerned over nothing. Brandon *was* on her side. "You know how much I've wanted to travel. It's the perfect solution." She gushed with excitement, her mind filling with images of Europe. "Where shall I go? Paris? Rome? I can take painting lessons in Florence. Perhaps Milan? I can see the great churches like Mama always dreamed of doing. I can make it a pilgrimage."

"Yerba Buena." Brandon dropped the foreign words into the one-sided conversation.

"Yerba Buena? Where's that?" The thought stymied Moira's imagination for only a moment. Perhaps it was in Spain. Spain held a mystery all its own. She could enjoy Spain. Spain was supposed to be warm and the Alhambra was there.

"It's a small settlement in Alta California on the West Coast."

"Why there?" she asked tentatively. The West Coast might as well be the moon, so far was it from New York in both distance and culture. There were no museums, no art, no opera, no shopping or parties. It was, in short, wilderness and a mostly unclaimed one at that.

"Because that is where your husband will be stationed with the American troops at the Presidio, the military enclave there protecting US interests." Brandon's gaze was unwavering.

It took a moment to process his words. They made no sense. "My *husband*? I don't have one." Did he mean for her to pick a man from the garrison there?

"Major Benjamin Sheffield has asked for your hand. Perhaps you recall him from the house party? He was there. Apparently, your antics didn't get his attention in the same way they got Mrs. Bostwick's. He rode over to speak with me this morning. I accepted on your behalf."

"This morning! You accepted on my behalf? You didn't think to consult me?" Moira grasped for the most comprehensible straws of this insane conversation. She wasn't sure what to focus on first; the horror of having a husband, the insult in not being consulted or the utter sense of betrayal that went with both. It was almost too much to take in.

Instead, she tried to recall who Major Sheffield

might have been and came up blank. There were men at the party who barely registered; men who'd rather talk business and politics in the corners instead of dance and participate in games like Phillip Hawley and Robert Umbridge. There was a group of young men who'd been too shy for her tastes; Elmer Murphy, Francis Nesbitt, James Cowan and others, *many* others. New York was so full of boring young men.

No one among its members struck her as being a major. The man her brother had offered her to was a military man, not a shy young man or a businessman. Perhaps a political man, though? She ran back through her images of the men gathered with Hawley and Umbridge. Had any of them appeared to have a military bearing? She couldn't recall. She hadn't paid enough attention, hadn't thought there was a reason to, and there still wasn't. Whatever her brother had done, she'd persuade him to undo it.

"You could have asked me. You *should* have asked me." Moira fixed him with a hard stare. "You had no right to give me away as if I were a thing." The more she thought about it, the more his action stung. Real tears began to form. "I can't believe you'd do such a thing, Brandon."

"Moira, please. This is for the best," her brother argued. "It's time to marry, time to settle down. It's what Mother and Father would want for you, happiness with a family. If Father were still alive, you'd be married already. I've waited too long, put it off too long and I've done you a disservice in the procrastinating, thinking things would naturally take their course." He was trying to make it seem like the latest scandal was his fault, that he'd somehow failed in his duty and now he was making amends. "I want this for you, Moira."

"What about what I want for myself?" Moira cried.

"What is that? Do you even know?" Brandon was sharp, perhaps sensing that his strategy of offering her the gift of a marriage was not selling well with her.

"Are you scolding me?" This was nearly as shocking as the announcement he'd found her a husband. He never scolded.

"Yes, I am, and high time, too." Some of the sharpness faded from his features. "This is as much my fault as it is yours. I've allowed you to run amok all these years. I've humored you when I should have scolded you."

That was too much. "You've been the best of brothers," she assured him, hurt that he thought of himself as a failure because of her choices. Brandon couldn't fail at anything no matter how hard he tried. He'd not led her into scandal after scandal, that was all her.

"Yet you are unwed and teetering on the brink of social disaster. Major Sheffield will give you the respectability of marriage, the protection of his name and a chance to travel, which I know you long to do." Brandon pressed his case gently. "Just think how you could thumb your nose at all the Mrs. Bostwicks of the world and prove them wrong when you end up with such a fine man." He ended with a soft chuckle.

It made her smile a little, but it didn't persuade her. "I'm not so petty as that. Pride goeth before a fall and such." Did Brandon think her so superficial that her head could be turned with such temptations? Marriage was forever, spite was short-lived. She wasn't going to marry the man just to thumb her nose at Mrs. Bostwick. She sighed and tried out a counterplan. "Perhaps I'll meet someone this winter or next summer even, at Saratoga. Would you like that?" Summer seemed eons off, having just ended, and Saratoga was full of wealthy cotton planters and their families escaping the humid Southern summers. Perhaps next year she'd smile at one of them. Perhaps. She wasn't sure she was in a hurry to marry. Brandon was right, there. She wasn't sure what she wanted.

Brandon shook his head, impervious to her attempt to outflank him. "No, not Saratoga. I think it must be Major Sheffield. I would not suggest this if I thought there was another option, or a better choice." There had been better choices when she'd first come out but she'd frightened them off. There'd been a baron's son from England even last year, but he'd been too quiet for her taste. She did *have* a taste, apparently, and it ran to the young bucks who stole kisses in the dark gardens behind the brightly lit ballrooms of New York's proper hostesses. Not that she'd ever marry one of them. She knew better than that, but in the interim, they were loads of good fun.

"Do you recall Major Sheffield from the party?" Brandon prompted.

"No, absolutely not." She racked her mind once more for some kind of remembrance. None came. Too bad he hadn't been in uniform. It would certainly have helped him stand out.

Brandon rose from the desk. "Well, it doesn't matter. You can refresh your memory. He's waiting in the sitting room to speak with you and discuss details."

Waiting? He was here? A foreboding sense of reality settled on her. There was no way out. There never had been even before she'd opened her mouth. There'd never been an argument that would have changed Brandon's mind. Everything had been decided without her. She was merely a pawn being traded between the two of them—her brother and a faceless man. *And there was nothing she could do about it.* The fight was over without ever having come to her, and she'd lost.

Moira felt as if she were being ushered to her execution as they made their way down the hall. She'd awakened this morning free of cares, and suddenly she was on the verge of her own wedding to a man she didn't know, but one who had impressed her brother enough to win his approval and whisk her away to the wilderness of Yerba Buena. To *exile.* All because of a little wildness in her.

As they neared the sitting room, Brandon pulled her aside and took her hands. "I've prayed on this, as Mother and Father taught us to do when faced with difficulty. I've prayed for you especially this past year. I've asked for the direction to guide you, to keep you from a dangerous path. The major is a godly man, Moira. Perhaps this is the direction I've been praying for and the direction you need, the path away from the destructive one you're on. Please, give him a chance. I would not have suggested it if I had misgivings." Her brother's words stung. He had no misgivings about the major, but apparently, he had plenty about *her*, his own sister. She'd disappointed him for the last time.

Moira nodded, some of her anger and outrage permuting into sadness and even a modicum of regret. He'd given her so much more than she'd given him in return. He'd been barely twenty when their parents died. He'd been instantly burdened with a shipping empire to sustain and a little sister to raise while he should have been traveling Europe and sowing wild oats like other young men his age. Yet, he'd never complained about having his life upended, never turned away from God. Her brother was so much better than she and it shamed her. When was the last time *she'd* prayed? Really prayed and sought God's will for her life? Yes, she bowed her head for grace at the table, yes, she attended worship on Sundays at Grace Church and sat dutifully beside Brandon and his wife. But meaningful private prayer? She'd given that up years ago.

Prayer had not done much for her. It had not saved Mama and Papa. Crisis after crisis had strengthened Brandon's faith but those same crises had weakened her own. What kind of God took a ten-year-old's parents?

Brandon didn't deserve to be brought down by her scandals, nor did he deserve to spend his life mopping them up. She could do this one thing he asked of her. "I will try, Brandon."

Her brother smiled, but there was no relief for her in it. Whether she tried or not, failed or not, succeeded or not, her future lay behind that door. It would be up to her to make the best of it whether she wanted to or not. She opened the door and drew a breath. *Here's hoping for a miracle,* she thought, although she knew she didn't deserve one.

Chapter Two

He stood by the window that overlooked her mother's rose garden, his back to her giving her a full view of broad shoulders, a narrow waist and long legs spread shoulder width apart, hands clasped firmly behind him. If his uniform hadn't given away his office, his stance would have. He might have been surveying his troops on parade instead of a rose garden. A military man and a religious man, according to her brother. Perhaps an odd combination on the surface, but both demanded discipline of will and stern, tenacious character. It begged the question, what did such a man want with her? Especially a man who'd seen her at the house party where her behavior had, admittedly, bordered on irreverent.

He turned from the window at the sound of her approach, an alert man, then, who was attuned to even the soft step of slippers on carpet and the slight susurration of muslin. But he did not smile, not even when she did. Most men smiled when they saw her. She remembered him now, the somber man who had indeed spent time with the older gentlemen discussing business, although seeing him now in uniform, she thought he didn't appear as if he naturally belonged to that set. He'd been in close conversation with the aging greengrocer Edgar Franks, who was seventy if he was a day, and the austere Lucas Fielding, who had a nose like a hawk's beak and dressed exclusively in black. The major had almost entirely devoted himself to the two men, attaching himself only briefly to Umbrage's group.

He was in his late thirties, no more. There was no late-night billiards games, or flirtations with the ladies. He had joined in with the competitions Mrs. Bostwick had arranged, and while he'd done better than anyone, he'd humbly not participated in the finals although he could have easily won. Really, he was not an exciting man at all.

"Major Sheffield?" She made him a small curtsy. "My brother tells me you'd like to speak with me." She could not put it more mildly than that.

The long dark blue coat of his uniform showed off his physique, a major's epaulets sat on broad shoulders, and his belt spanned a trim waist. His head was bare, showing off wavy but carefully styled golden hair and somber blue eyes. Everything about him was careful and somber, from his eyes to the immaculate brushed sheen of his uniform, and even his speech, every word considered and measured. He gestured toward the chintz-covered settee set before the fire.

"Perhaps we might sit and talk." He was a cool one, so calm as he began the process of proposing matrimony to a woman he hardly knew.

"Your brother might have told you something about my purpose in calling upon you. I am looking for a wife to accompany me and my two daughters to my posting in Yerba Buena."

Two daughters? Her brother had forgotten to mention that. She was expected to be an immediate wife and a mother to a strange family she didn't know. But where a more timid person might be subdued by the prospect, Moira saw an opening to argue her case. "I am hardly maternal, as you so aptly saw at the house party. A pistol-shooting hoyden is hardly likely to be a demure role model for impressionable girls. I am not your best choice, there, Major, I assure you."

"Quite the opposite, in fact. That little display convinced me utterly you were the one. I had nearly given up hope of finding anyone suitable until I saw you taking on the boastful Edward Brant." The briefest of smiles whispered at his mouth and then disappeared. This was perhaps the closest she would get to a courtship from him, this impeccable, practical, somber man who'd not wasted a moment in dressing up the proposal as anything remotely romantic. At least he was honest. She could respect that.

"You want to marry me for my shooting abilities? I'm sure I'm flattered, Major." She held his gaze, not bothering to feign demureness or to put on an act to please him. She would be honest, too. He needed to be aware of what he was getting. Honesty was her last best defense in the hopes that he would rethink his proposal.

"No, you're not. You're not flattered in the least. You are horrified at the sudden curtailing of your freedoms and putting a brave face on it, while you attempt to talk me out of it, having failed to do so, no doubt, with your brother. I understand and admire that very much. Such tenacity will serve you well where I'm going." His own gaze did not waver, nor did he attempt to smile again to take the edge off his own honesty. He gave every impression of being a stern but fair man. A strict man, too, a man of discipline. He might have been impressed with her shooting and tenacity, but he would not allow her to cross him without penalty.

"Now that you've made your case, Miss Blackthorne, allow me to make mine in order to ease your misgivings about heading into a strange land with a strange man. I've been a professor at West Point these last several years. When the call came for the establishment of the First Volunteers to go to Yerba Buena, I felt it offered a way to serve both my country and myself."

He offered another brief smile, this one rueful, and Moira saw a hint of sadness surface in his eyes. Ah, so this stern, organized, straightforward man was capable of emotion, too. Perhaps that meant he'd be forgiving when she inevitably would cross his strict lines of protocol. "I'm looking for a fresh start, you see," he began. "My wife died three years ago and since then, my position at West Point has lost its appeal. It will do the girls and me good to start again somewhere new."

He'd chosen well, there, then. One could not get any "newer" than California.

Her thoughts must have shown on her face. He gave a short laugh and rushed to reassure her. "You needn't worry over your comfort. I'm an officer in the United States army. It affords me the luxury of providing you and my daughters with a home, a real home at the Presidio once we arrive. You will not live in tents or barracks. The girls need a steadying presence since I am often gone and they need teaching. I won't have my girls grow up to be uneducated misses nor simpering ones."

"Hence the need for a crack shot as a wife." Moira couldn't resist the sharp barb. She wasn't convinced the major had read her right. Tenacity wasn't a quality that usually recommended one for wife-hood. Tenacious wives were difficult wives, or so society liked to preach. Brandon may not have mentioned children but the major had mentioned them twice now in short succession. They were important to him and obviously not far from his mind as he made his plans.

"How old are your daughters?" Moira asked. It was becoming clear to her what drove the major's proposal. He wanted a mother for his children more than a wife for himself.

He smiled at her question and this time it transformed his face. His blue eyes crinkled at the corners. "Margaret, Maggie for short, is thirteen, and

Elizabeth, or Lizzie, is nine." He paused before saying quietly, "I fear at this time in their lives, without their mother, they are very much alone. They have my mother, of course, but she is an older woman. It's been a long time since she was a young girl with a young girl's dreams and fears."

Or a young girl's grief. Moira nodded her understanding. Three years or twelve years, grief had no statute of limitations. Her parents might have died yesterday so raw did her own grief feel at times. Another thought came to her. "You needn't marry me to have a governess or companion for them." A flicker of hope sprang to life. Perhaps this was the compromise? Perhaps she could convince the major to take her along but then allow her to return to New York once the girls were settled?

"Certainly not, Miss Blackthorne." The major fixed her with his stern gaze. "Aboard a ship for six months is no place for an unmarried woman no matter how good of a shot she is. And my girls need more than a governess. They need a mother, they need permanence. This move is no small upheaval for them. They need someone they can count on to be there."

The stern words overwhelmed her as nothing else had. When had anyone counted on her? Relied on her? "I am honored you would entrust their care to me, although I am still somewhat surprised given the conditions under which I came to your notice." What did she know of mothering? Of childrearing? Surely, her demonstration at Mrs. Bostwick's should have disqualified her from such consideration. She very much feared the major would only be disappointed in her.

"Quite the contrary. My daughters will need a firm hand. They need someone who can stand up *to* them and *for* them if the need arises. You did not back down from a challenge and you were passionate in your defense of your ability, even if a bit misguided. Winning isn't everything. I can only imagine how you would defend a child under your protection." He shook his head, stalling her protest that shooting contests and children were hardly the same thing.

"People rise to the occasion required of them, Miss Blackthorne," he continued. "I have no doubts you will do the same. Yerba Buena will provide quite the outlet for your energy and determination. In addition to managing my home and daughters, there are settlers and natives to become accustomed to. Yerba Beuna is not New York. You will be busy."

In other words, she would not have time to get into trouble.

The major wasn't finished. "When I am done with the military, I hope to invest in a business as the situation permits. Greengrocery seems a likely avenue to pursue as the settlement grows. People need a place to buy fresh food and farmers need a place to sell it."

Well, that explained why he'd spent so much time with Fielding and Franks, two of the guests who'd spent the party talking business with the major and other men. They'd made a fortune in New York with greengrocery.

More than that, however, she understood what his pronouncement meant. There would be no turning back. Yerba Buena was to be their permanent home. This was not a temporary venture. Perhaps in the far-off future, they might return to New York when the girls were of an age to be launched into society, but it was a long, arduous trip either around Cape Horn and several months at sea or overland by wagon. Maybe that was her brother's hope; that by the time she returned to New York, she would be tamed, a dutiful officer's wife or shopkeeper's wife, perhaps with children of her own or perhaps not? If he was looking for a mother for his children, he might not want any more. The thought prompted her next question, bold and impertinent as it was. Mrs. Bostwick would faint dead away if she heard her ask it.

"What of yourself in this arrangement, Major? What do you get out of all of this?" Children of her own implied certain things she'd need to do with the major, a stranger.

"A mother for my children, and perhaps in time a helpmate for myself, someone who will enjoy running my home. Perhaps a friend as we come to know each other. That is all, Miss Blackthorne." He held her gaze steady as he said the words.

"Why do you think I would accept your offer? Why would I want to leave all of this, the wealth of my brother's house, the luxuries of city living, summers in Saratoga, winters in Florida, for the heat and difficulties of the West, not to mention war? I am sure 'difficulties' is an understatement for what awaits out there." Everyone had so carefully avoided the mention that the United States was currently at war with Mexico and that the California territory was no small part of that.

"Because there are opportunities to claim the territory peacefully for the country through settlement," he corrected. "I will tell you why you'll accept, Miss Blackthorne." His tone was even and stern. "You are bored here, running from near-scandal to near-scandal in the hopes that something will inflame some passion in you, some reason for living, and nothing does. It will be the ruin of you. It is just a matter of time before you go too far for your brother to redeem you. I offer you the redemption of marriage, the adventure you crave and a chance to carve out a place for yourself on your terms. California is a blank slate, waiting for you to write on it. You will not get a better offer."

How was it that this man knew her so well on such short acquaintance? She found it uncomfortable to be stripped bare, to have someone see so clearly into her heart, perhaps even better than she did herself. She *was* bored. Bored and angry; angry with herself, angry for failing to live up to her brother's expectations; angry with the world that found no place for her high spirits; angry at a God who'd allowed her parents to die. Was that all there was to the world? Anger? Rage? The futility of struggle? And here sat a man who offered her a way out, perhaps not a way out of her anger, but at least a way out of her boredom and a way to please her brother after all he'd done for her. He had hit the nail on the head: What was there for her here but ruin and her brother's disappointment? Her brother wanted this and she'd done very little that he'd wanted in the last twelve years.

She straightened. "Very well, Major Sheffield. I accept your offer." As if that acceptance had ever been in question. Perhaps it was some small insight into his character that he had not immediately reminded her of that. He'd offered her this small opportunity to save face.

His only response was to offer a short nod. "I thank you for the honor, Miss Blackthorne. We can be wed tomorrow."

"Tomorrow!" Moira exclaimed. "I can't possibly be wed tomorrow, there's a wedding to plan, and packing, and arrangements to be made." One could not decamp to farthest Yerba Buena without provisions.

"Yes, I understand completely. Forgive my haste. I forget how women like to pack and plan. You may have four days to make your preparations."

Four days? She wanted to protest even that, but she could see from the softening look on his face that he thought this was a great mercy. She didn't dare ask for more. "Oh my, Major, you are eager to wed indeed." Perhaps if she fished very carefully for an explanation he would give one, especially since he'd been the one to suggest this be a marriage in name only. Romance was not behind his speedy agenda.

"I am eager to make the ship on time," he offered. "We sail on the twenty-sixth." He gave her a small bow. "Make your preparations. I shall return the day after tomorrow with the girls so that you may meet them and we all might shop together for what they need. That will allow you a day to make your lists and your plans." One day to plan a wedding and pack for a voyage that would take her across the continent, months away from her family.

"You're leaving?" She'd almost missed that piece of information, so distracted was she over the other piece of news: they were essentially to go from the wedding to the ship. There would only be the interval of a night between the ceremony and departure. She would have to acclimate herself to a new husband, a new family and a new life all at once. "I had thought we might use these four days to get to know one another better." There would be no time for that. Even when he returned, the girls would be with him.

He shook his blond head. "I do apologize for the haste, but my men await my instructions. The regiments ship out on the twenty-sixth. Do not worry. We have a whole voyage to get to know one another."

"Isn't that a bit backward? Getting to know each other *after* the wedding?" Moira didn't hesitate to argue.

He gave a wry smile. "That is quite often the way in the military—things done backward. But needs must prevail. The men must be on board the twenty-third. It's a marvel I've been allowed a pass off the boat for the wedding arrangements at all. We must be on board as soon as possible on the twenty-fifth. So you see, the twenty-fourth is really the latest we can manage."

That meant a whole day just sitting in the harbor. It seemed a waste of time to her. Moira wasn't sure how she felt about having her schedule dictated by someone—something—other than herself. "Yes, of course," Moira said, although she didn't. She'd been born the daughter of a wealthy shipping magnate, and she was the sister of one in turn. Hers was not a military background. She'd been raised to a life of freedoms and privileges whether she knew it or not. Her days were not spent at the beck and call of another.

He gave her another small, short-lived smile. "I am glad you do. An officer's wife is someone the other women can look to for leadership and direction. If you will excuse me, I must see to my troops this afternoon. I've already been away longer than I would have liked."

Moira stayed seated long after Major Sheffield left, the enormity of what had occurred keeping her rooted in place. Perhaps if she stayed in one spot time would be frozen, the wedding would never come. But if she moved, time would start again, an exorable march toward Saturday, her wedding. There would be no engagement party, no four-day courtship, no marriage trip. Just a ceremony to make the marriage legal. It was certainly not the stuff of romance and fairy tale. This was barebones practicality.

A soft knock at the door announced Brandon's arrival. "Major Sheffield has given me the details," he offered tentatively. "He's a good man, Moira. I think you can find some happiness with him, if you try." Brandon dusted his hands against his thighs.

"Four days is not a lot of time. We'll help you with packing. Gemma already has the footmen getting the trunks out of the attics."

Trunks. A reminder that she was not packing for a journey but for a lifetime. When would she see her home again? That was a whole new level of enormity that was just beginning to overtake her. "You're sending me away." She couldn't keep the accusation out of her voice. When would she see Brandon and Gemma and little Ethan again? Apparently, the enormity of this change just kept coming, just kept rolling over her in Atlantic-sized waves.

"I am giving you a chance at a new life," Brandon corrected gently. He took her hands and drew her to him in a brotherly hug, more like his old self. "You are wasted on stuffy old New York, my dear girl. You need a new land, a new place where there's room for you."

She sniffed and looked up at him. "Do you remember what you said about me getting to rub everyone's noses in it?"

"Yes, and you said you were above that." Brandon chuckled.

"Well, I'm not so far above it, short notice or not. If I am leaving New York, I'm not skulking out of here in the middle of the night. Mrs. Bostwick and her cronies are going to have to give me a sendoff." She gave a tremulous smile trying hard not to cry. She never cried, not anymore, not since she realized tears couldn't change a thing. They couldn't bring Mother and Father back and they couldn't stop this wedding. "Bran, I am going to want a wedding. The best the neighbors have ever seen. Grace Church and everything."

She had her pride, after all. Major Sheffield was in a hurry to wed only because haste suited him and his regiment. It certainly did not flatter her. He'd come to Mrs. Bostwick's house party to find a wife from among his social connections. He'd been on a mission and it was clear he'd looked upon that mission the same way he likely looked upon a military task. He wanted a wife and he was not going to sail without one. He'd been determined to pick a bride from whatever was on offer at the house party and she came the closest to what he needed—someone who could hold her own whether with his daughters, onboard the ship or once at Yerba Buena.

Being chosen was hardly a compliment when she thought of the other girls who'd been there, all silly frilly debutantes dressed in white. She couldn't imagine any of *them* surviving the uncivilized California wilderness. Apparently, neither could he. Major Sheffield had picked her. He might not know her, but he'd liked her tenacity—enough to wager his life and hers on it. It made one wonder just what sort of man Benjamin Sheffield was beneath the starched and pressed uniform and commitment to duty above all else. Beneath that surface lingered a different kind of man, a thought that was as exciting to the adventurer in her as it was unsettling to the girl who'd never left home.

Chapter Three

What kind of man proposed marriage just days before shipping out? Ben didn't allow himself to ponder a potential answer to that question until he was safely returned to Governor's Island, where the regiment was installed and he was ensconced in the manly preserve of what passed for an officer's club in camp. Didn't just propose, but proposed to a woman he barely knew.

Someone came to take his order; cider, the usual. Especially in the summer and early fall when the air was still warm, there was nothing like a tankard of cold cider to wet the throat and settle the mind. Tonight, he needed both. He'd not actually spoken to her, to *Moira*—she had a name—until this afternoon. At the house party, he'd only watched her from across the drawing room, or from the other end of the table.

Even at a distance with his sightline often inter-

rupted by the intrusion of others, he'd not been able
to take his eyes from her. She was life itself, a vi-
vacious flame that drew everyone into its orbit. She
didn't ask for attention, didn't beg for it or crave
it like many of the girls, and yet attention found
her anyway. Perhaps it was her appearance that ac-
counted for it. She was slightly taller than the other
girls, slightly older. Simply put, she was slightly *more*
than all of them; more confident, more determined,
more outspoken. All that vivacity drew a man; made
a man want to cross a room, to stand in the penumbra
of her light, made a man believe he, too, could come
to life if he could just get close enough.

Fanciful as the thought was, he hadn't been the
only man present thinking it. She was never alone,
as evidenced by the collection of well-dressed moths
circling her flame. They were the wrong sorts, of
course; reckless scions of New York's finest families,
young men with more money than sense. They could
afford to be reckless. She couldn't by the very nature
of her gender. Watching her flirt with them, laugh
with them, goad them on, was a reminder that the
line between *being* trouble or being *in* trouble was
thin, and Moira Blackthorne might be both. There
were those—his hostess, Mrs. Bostwick, included—
who did not find Miss Blackthorne a worthy candi-
date for his post. A wife to a grief-struck widower,
a surrogate mother to two half-grown girls, needed
to be a woman of great refinement. She would be in
charge of raising and educating two girls who might

eventually return to New York and take their place in society.

His cider came and Ben took a long, cold swallow. Miss Blackthorne's behavior did not recommend her as someone to fill that role in the eyes of the Mrs. Bostwicks. And yet, he'd been drawn to her, no different from the other swains, except in one respect. He thought he might understand her better, thanks to the vantage of his thirty plus years.

Another swallow, another cold, bracing draught of clarity. This was not love at first sight. He had seen too much and lost too much in life to put store by such a frivolous concept any longer. But she did stir something in him; a flickering, an awakening he could barely name but knew he needed, something his little motherless family had lacked these past years. His one thought was that perhaps she—Moira Blackthorne with her inky dark waves and flashing eyes—could give it back to them.

He'd just arrived at the thought when she'd challenged Edward Brant to the shootout and the other piece of his puzzling attraction fell into place: she needed them as much as he and the girls needed her. Hers was an audacity born of boredom and it would lead to her ruin. There was no place in staid New York society for her. These young men who flirted with her now would not marry her. But he would. He could give his girls a mother who would endure and he could give Moira Blackthorne a chance if she was bold enough to take it.

And that was his answer. Ben nursed his cider,

rolling the answer around in his mind. What sort of man married a woman he barely knew? A man who wanted to live again, who was tired of feeling dead inside, as if he, too, had been buried with his wife, a man who wanted his daughters to laugh again. It was the very same reason he'd signed on for the mission to California. He wanted a fresh start.

"You're safely returned from society's clutches, I see." Cortland Visser, a fellow officer assigned to H Company, strolled up and helped himself to the other chair. He pulled it close for privacy, his eyes glancing on the tankard. "Are celebrations in order?" he asked quietly, referring to Ben's mission.

He felt a small smile form. "Yes, matter of fact, they are. I am to be married." Saying the words aloud to another added a layer of reality to what he'd done, and it also served as a reminder that in some ways this act wasn't as precipitous as he made it out to be.

"Your mission to Mrs. Bostwick's was successful." Cort's eyes were merry. "I knew it would be. You've never failed at anything since I've known you back in our West Point days as cadets. You've achieved anything you set your mind to." He laughed and reached over to clap him on the shoulder. "You're the only man I know who can go to a house party and come home with a wife in tow. You must have impressed her."

"Something like that." He downed a large swallow of cider instead of answering more directly. The truth was, her brother had been impressed. She'd been impressed in a very different way, more akin to the way the British once "impressed" men into the navy.

"Well?" Cort persisted when he offered no other information about his abrupt courtship. "What are your plans? When is the wedding?"

That was easier to talk about. He'd always been a plans man, an action man. Action took the focus of emotion and sentiment. "The girls will arrive in town tomorrow. They'll stay at my uncle's in Manhattan. The day after, I'll take them to meet her and we'll take care of shopping. The next day is the wedding and then we sail." To a new land, a new life.

Cort slapped his leg. "You're so cool about it all, laying it out like a military campaign. But I'm not surprised. You've approached it like a campaign from the start, the 'intelligence' from your mother about the house party, the guest list, the timeline. Now all that's left is provisioning and you've got that taken care of as well." Cort tossed him a wry smile. "It's very efficient but not terribly romantic."

He thought of Moira's blunt questions and answers this afternoon. It hadn't been a proposal as much as it had been an acceptance of a surrender cloaked as a negotiation to save Moira Blackthorne's rather considerable pride. Romance wasn't a consideration. "This isn't a love match. This is about filling a position in my household, a position my girls desperately need. She understands what she's signing up for."

Cort chuckled, unconvinced. "If you say so. Let me know how that works out for you. A lady, any lady, might grow tired of being thought of as a campaign. A little romance on occasion wouldn't go amiss. Just some advice." Cort winked.

"Advice from a sworn bachelor?" Ben laughed and settled into his chair, starting to relax. The deed was done. His daughters would be here tomorrow, the fresh start he longed for was just days away. He had accomplished what he'd set out to do. Thinking of it in those terms was far less nerve wracking than thinking about the enormity of what he was committing to. Perhaps such callousness did the institution of marriage a disservice but sometimes a soldier did what he must to get through to the next stage.

His conscience gave him a hard pricking, unwilling to let him overlook other reasons for the callousness. Perhaps that callousness served other purposes as well, protecting and preserving other memories, other times, when marriage was more than a position, when there'd been more to life than duty to country and others. A little ribbon of whisper wound through his thoughts. Perhaps those times might come again if he allowed it. He would not let himself go running headlong down that path, and *if* he did explore that path, it would not be at a run but at a cautious walk, fully aware of what was at stake and what he could lose.

He pushed the thought away and changed the subject. "What is the news here? Has anything more come of the Sutherland issue?" A little over two weeks ago, a man who'd been denied a spot in the regiment by Colonel Stevenson, the director of the entire operation, had threatened Stevenson with the loss of his command.

Cort blew out a breath, gathering himself for a tale. "An informant from the sheriff's office brought news that Sutherland has men willing to bring charges against the colonel over false imprisonment on the grounds the physical examinations were delayed upon their arrival. They are suing for financial damages amounting to eighty thousand dollars."

"What nonsense." Ben shook his head. "There's no meat to it. The physicians had more men to examine than anticipated. It simply wasn't possible to get through them any faster." Men reporting for potential enlistment in Stevenson's regiment had been promised examination and placement within four days of their arrival on Governor's Island. That had not been a promise that could be kept. As a result, over one hundred and fifty men were kept on Governor's Island until the end of August only to learn they were not in acceptable shape for the regiment. Most had understood the situation but Sutherland had found a core of men who were willing to protest the situation with charges.

Cort shrugged. "There's enough meat for the sheriff's office to issue warrants against Stevenson. That's where things stand now. The warrants are issued but they are meaningless until they're served. But if they were served, they could prevent him from sailing, perhaps prevent all of us from sailing if the head of the expedition isn't able to go." That was worrisome. Ben was not in general a huge fan of the pompous, self-styled Stevenson, but he didn't want the voyage canceled or postponed, not now when he'd pushed for a hasty marriage and dragged the girls to Manhattan from West Point.

"Has Stevenson boarded his ship?" Ben could see where this chess game was going. It was a race against the clock now.

Cort nodded. "Yes, along with his men. No one is to board otherwise. No one is to get close enough to him to serve those warrants. Then we sail on the twenty-sixth and the warrants will have no power."

"I suppose Stevenson is regretting not sailing on the twenty-fifth." The colonel had originally wanted to sail Friday, but the men had been superstitious about the departure date and Stevenson had diplomatically switched the date. For himself, Ben appreciated the extra day. He would have been hardpressed to wed and make the boat on the twenty-fourth with his girls and his bride.

"Maybe. But all will be well. Stevenson will be protected," Cort chuckled.

"What of his daughters?" Ben asked with concern. Stevenson's girls were motherless like his own. It was one of the things he and the colonel had in common, both were widowers with children. Unlike himself, though, Stevenson was not bringing his girls with him.

Cort dropped his voice. "He rowed ashore near midnight once his crew boarded the *Thomas Perkins*. He was able to secretly meet with them for a few hours and say goodbye."

Ben nodded his approval. He didn't particularly like Stevenson. The man was overly fond of himself, but Ben did not wish him ill. Stevenson had had a hard time of it since announcing he was forming the regiment. "And the men, how are they?" August had been long and hot and several men had learned too late they didn't have the stamina or the stomach for military life. It had been the work of the summer to turn the volunteers into soldiers. A West Pointer like himself knew that such discipline didn't come easy or early. It was the product of hardship and time. Still, progress had been made even if there was still more to make.

"As well as can be expected," Cort offered. "At least the desertions have stopped now that the men are aboard the boats." Despite the flood of applicants early on, the companies were now undermanned. Ben didn't mind. It was best those men who couldn't handle the voyage and life in the wilderness declare themselves now lest they become dead weight later on.

Ben finished his cider and rose. "I'm off to bed. Tomorrow will be busy." And the next two days busier. He had correspondence to see to, including a note to his bride that he and his daughters would call on her at eleven in the morning on September 23 in order to make introductions and to engage in shopping. He thought the last was inspired. Shopping was always a good way for women to start relationships.

September 23, 1846

Her husband-to-be was a punctual man. Major Benjamin Sheffield and his daughters, Margaret and Elizabeth, arrived at the brownstone mansion promptly at eleven. Moira's hands clenched in her skirts as the butler announced them, the stroke of the hall clock having barely died away. She could have done with a little less promptness, and a few more minutes to gather herself perhaps. Although in truth, a few minutes more would not make a difference. She was as ready as she'd ever be to meet her fiancé and his daughters. She'd been "gathering" herself the moment Major Sheffield had left the town house two days ago. Moira cast a fleeting look in her sister-in-law's' direction and gave the nod to the butler. "Send them in, Steadings."

Gemma flashed her a smile. "Just be yourself, my dear. The girls will love you as much as your little nephew does." Moira wanted to argue that it was hardly the same. Ethan couldn't even walk yet. What did he know? These girls were half-grown, one thirteen, and one eight. She remembered herself at eight *and* at thirteen. She'd had plenty of opinions and been in plenty of scrapes, stealing boys' clothes from swimming holes and looking for ways to get out of lessons. It was a wonder her parents hadn't despaired of her when they were alive, and later her brother.

She'd been doing a lot of that—remembering—since Tuesday, not just what it had been like to be a girl of that age, but remembering those around her.

How had they coped with her? She found herself wondering what her mother had done. What would her mother tell her to do if she were here now? The woman had been a paragon, all that was patient and kind, good and honorable, always putting others and family above self. *If she'd been more selfish she might still be alive* came the unworthy rejoinder. Her mother would be ashamed of such a thought. She would know exactly what to do with two motherless girls. It was just another mental jab as to how unlike her mother she was. Suffice it to say, her saint of a mother would never have found herself in such a situation.

There was a rustle in the hall announcing the arrival of her company. Moira rose, smoothing the skirts of her black-and-white wide-spaced tartan plaid, a gown more white than black for summer. She fussed with the lace fichu at her neck, adjusting the cameo that held it in place. Her sister-in-law squeezed her hand and whispered encouragingly, "You look lovely."

"Major Sheffield, Mrs. Ellen Sheffield and the major's daughters," Steadings intoned. For a moment, the reference threw her. *Mrs.* Sheffield? Of course. The children's grandmother. The lady in question was a vigorous woman of seventy with sharp blue eyes like her son, the major. *The major*—would she always think of him that way? Or should she start to think of him as Benjamin or even Ben?—looked different today. He'd not, she realized, worn his uniform, but was dressed instead in a dark blue frock coat with a blue plaid waistcoat beneath and cream trousers, his glossy blond hair combed to one side in a golden wave. He looked somehow younger and less severe than he had on his first visit. Perhaps his daughters had a softening effect on him.

The girls flanked him on either side. The oldest, Margaret, on his left, a blond-haired miss of thirteen turned out in a pale blue dress that showed off her blue eyes. Margaret was on course to being a beauty. On his right dressed in pink and ruffles was Lizzie, dark-haired and snub-nosed with freckles that spoke of time in the sun. What lovely, biddable girls they seemed. Every inch of them was perfection from the curls in their hair to their neatly ironed dresses.

"I am so pleased to meet you both," Moira said as their grandmother gestured for the girls to come forward and make their curtsies—a perfunctory, polite gesture done by rote. Afterward, they looked awkwardly at their grandmother for direction, who gave them a nod of approval.

Moira wished there was more to say, perhaps that their father had told her so much about them, but she would not begin their relationship with a lie. Beyond names and ages, their father had said nothing at all. Suddenly, a riot of questions filled her. What did they like to eat? Did they have favorite sweets? What did they like to do? Did they ride? Or read? Her mother's voice spoke calmly in her head: *It will come, all in good time. For all things there is a season.*

Moira cast about for something to say, something to interest them. "Do you like to shop?" she asked the girls, searching their eyes for a sign of interest, a sign of welcome. Their gaze darted to their grandmother. Undaunted, Moira forged ahead, infusing her voice. "I've been making lists and lists of things we shall need—clothes, and household items, puzzles and books. The list is ever so long. But I'll need your help selecting items that are to your taste." Moira smiled at the girls conspiratorially, but it was Mrs. Sheffield who answered.

"I have supplied their father with a list of items they'll need." The older woman's sharp eyes raked over her in appraisal. Apparently, she was not pleased with her son's decision to marry, or perhaps the decision to marry her specifically. Moira bristled under the woman's unspoken censure. She knew a gauntlet when it was thrown.

"Perhaps our lists will complement one another, then." Moira flashed the girls a dazzling smile. "Two lists are better than one. Twice the shopping." Shopping she hoped Mrs. Sheffield would not insinuate herself into. When she'd imagined this shopping expedition, she'd not pictured the major's mother tagging along.

Gemma came to her assistance, showing off the hostessing skills that had impressed Moira's brother during their courtship. Since then, she'd taken her place among the ranks for New York's most fashionable young matrons, a hostess superb. "Mrs. Sheffield, it is so good of you to accompany the girls. Perhaps you would stay to tea with me and our two families can become acquainted." She looped an arm through Mrs. Sheffield's before the woman could voice an argument.

Moira stepped forward toward the girls. "Now that's settled, shall we get on with our excursion? I dare say we'll run your father off his feet." She flashed another smile, this one at the major. "Where shall we start? I suggest A. T. Stewart's store, and if we're lucky we can finish there as well. They have positively everything a girl could want." Except freedom, Moira thought ruefully. That one commodity seemed to be in short supply these days.

Chapter Four

A brief trill of victory shot through Moira as they stepped into Stewart's Department Store. She'd chosen well. The promise of a single stop for errands had appealed to the major, and the soaring four stories of Stewart's with its seventy-foot-wide domed rotunda appealed to the girls, whose eyes had grown wider as they'd approached the Tuckahoe marble facade of the store that dominated the two hundred block of Broadway.

"It's only recently opened," she told the girls, "but the *Herald* calls it 'the most splendid dry goods store in the world.'" The *Herald* also called it a divine place where women could while away their leisure hours, but such a thought probably bordered on blasphemous for the major, who didn't strike her as a man who tolerated idleness let alone the idleness that prompted leisurely spending.

The major held the door for them. "Best enjoy

it today, girls, there aren't stores like this in Yerba Buena." He smiled as they passed but Moira thought she sensed an undernote of disapproval.

"Think of it as provisioning, Major, if shopping offends you," she teased. If he found shopping distasteful, he ought not have chosen a wife from among society. It was just about all a young lady of quality was raised to do aside from a bit of archery and looking pretty in her dresses. Which was why she'd learned to shoot. It was far more interesting.

They started with shoes, moved on to house goods, and then to fabrics and linen, the major trailing behind them watching, assessing, his gaze guarded. It was hard to know who was most out of their depth here; him, trying to look comfortable shopping, or her, trying to tackle her lists with two girls in tow who seemed to have only two phrases in their vocabulary. "Yes, ma'am" and "Grandmother says…"

The former was not said with agreement but with reticence and the latter—"grandmother says"—presaged what Moira was coming to recognize as covert disagreement. If she suggested one color of fabric for a dress, Maggie was quick to say, "Grandmother says dark blue is more sensible for girls my age." Maggie was also quick to speak for Lizzie, Moira noted. "Grandmother prefers Lizzie in pink until she's ten. Grandmother prefers Lizzie and I not eat sweets." Although this was said rather ruefully when they passed the candy counter and Moira suggested a bag of gumdrops. "It rots the teeth, don't you know?"

Maggie explained politely. On the surface, there was nothing to find fault with the girl. But it was clear to Moira that what she'd mistaken for biddability at the outset was in truth a form of resistance.

"Not if you brush them." Moira tossed her a smile and purchased a bag anyway. She tried to cajole the girl into enjoying the treat. Lizzie looked as if she could be tempted but Maggie shot her sister a stern glance and staunchly refused for both of them. Moira coached herself to patience. One day couldn't undo three years of grief and now, perhaps just as the world had started to right itself, the girls' world had tilted again with this voyage. Maggie was stubborn and loyal perhaps not only to her grandmother but perhaps to a mother who was gone and about to be replaced.

The pile of fabrics on the counter was high and the afternoon was closing in on four o'clock. They were nearly done when the girls drifted off to a nearby counter while the last lengths were cut and the major settled the bill. Moira followed them. "What are you looking at?" The girls were pointing and sighing animatedly over whatever was in the case.

"Satin ribbons, aren't they divine?" It was the first genuine thing Moira had heard Maggie say all day and it came out in a breathy sigh. "There's slippers to match. I think when I'm grown up I'll make Cinderella blue my signature color, like Titian did with ultramarine." Ah, that was revealing, too. Maggie liked to paint.

"And I'll make mine green, like the color of spring grass." Lizzie copied her sister's sigh.

"Those are beautiful colors," Moira agreed, signaling for a clerk, hope stirring. Perhaps hair ribbons could be a bridge between them, a fun memory to mark the outing and the first day they met.

"Yes, miss, how can I help?" The clerk was eagerness. She felt someone come up behind her. The clerk's gaze moved beyond her shoulder. The major had arrived. Even in a woman's domain like Stewart's, a man's presence could usurp a woman's power.

"What are we looking at here?" the major asked his girls in friendly tones.

"Satin ribbons, Father, and slippers. Aren't they beautiful?" Maggie was all wide-eyed adolescent wistfulness.

"They are beautiful," the major agreed. "But they are impractical. You have plenty of hair ribbons that are sturdy and will endure where we are going. Besides, when would you wear them aboard ship or around the base?" The reminder was not meanly said. He'd not scolded the girls for looking at the fripperies but he had put paid to any consideration of purchasing.

Moira looked at their disappointed faces. She stepped close to the major, a hand at his sleeve, and said quietly, "Perhaps that's the very reason to indulge in something pretty. Something as simple as a colorful hair ribbon can brighten one's day when all seems dreary. The girls will be far from home, far from the usual comforts."

The major's gaze froze the rest of her argument, his own voice filled with quiet authority. "Miss Blackthorne, are you contradicting me in front of my daughters? In public?"

"No, certainly not. I was merely stating my opinion in the hopes you might reconsider." She would not allow herself to be intimidated nor would she give way simply to make a good impression on her future husband. This was who she was. Best he come to terms with that now. Not that he would back out. Her brother had announcements run yesterday in both the *Herald* and the *Tribune*.

The major gave her a curt nod. "Your opinion has been noted. I stand by my decision. I will not be purchasing satin ribbons and fanciful slippers for the girls to wear to California. I will not spoil my daughters."

No. Perhaps *he* wouldn't. But perhaps she would. He'd said nothing against her purchasing the items. She'd been thinking all day what might she purchase as Christmas gifts. They'd be at sea in December, a long way from home and still a long way from their destination. Ribbons might be just the thing. They were small and they'd take up little room in her luggage. She would come back for them. With that decided, it was easier to stand down on the issue. But she did wonder how many other issues her new husband might require her to stand down on and if she would. It wasn't in her nature and she didn't intend to change.

She turned back to the girls. Had they guessed at

the conversation? She was eager to appease their long faces and perhaps win back some temporarily gained favor. "Shopping has made me famished. Perhaps we might stop for tea? There's a place around the corner that serves delightful cream cakes."

"Oh, Father, can we? Tea in the city, just imagine it!" Maggie begged earnestly while Lizzie clapped her hands and promised to be on her best behavior.

The major smiled his approval, perhaps out of a need to compromise, or because he saw the merit in being a benevolent victor. Moira smiled back over the tops of the girls' heads, her sense of disappointment over his refusal of the ribbons easing. That was a good sign. She could appreciate a man with standards, but she would not tolerate a tyrant.

The tearoom was a safe harbor of genteel femininity amid the masculine sea of the city, and Ben immediately felt out of place. Delicate lace curtains shielded guests from the view of noisy Broadway. Wallpaper of pink roses and green vines set off with copious amounts of pristine white wainscoting and decorated at intervals with brass wall sconces made the restaurant feel like a woman's parlor. Indeed, it was populated as such. Each white-clothed table was filled with three or four well-dressed ladies chatting leisurely over teapots and teacups painted with violets and pansies, a five-tiered tray holding cakes and tiny sandwiches set in the table's center.

He felt as if every pair of eyes in the place followed the progress of his party to a quiet table in the corner, or perhaps those eyes were only watching him, their gazes drawn to the anomaly of a man in their midst, and perhaps an unwelcome anomaly at that. He was very much the intruder and he itched to be back outside, on the sidewalks crowded with passersby and the shouts of men as wagons jockeyed for position in the traffic. That was saying something, given that he far preferred the quiet of the Hudson Valley to the racket of the city.

The four of them took their seats at the table and Miss Blackthorne—*Moira*—ordered, tea for the two of them and the treat of hot chocolate for the girls. Maggie and Lizzie were looking about, just as wide-eyed here as they had been at Stewart's. Of the four of them, Moira was the only one in her element. This was her world, a world of shopping, of taking tea in a public shop, of navigating a bustling city with comfortable ease. It was a telling divide between them—all of them and her. His daughters had been raised in the bucolic Hudson Valley. Their lives had been simple. They were country girls. Miss Blackthorne was definitely not a country girl. She was a city girl born and bred.

How would she manage in the world into which he was taking her? There were no cities there. Not yet at least. Colonel Stevenson had aspirations to build a city to rival New York but that would not happen overnight; that would be the work of decades. Doubts assailed him once more. What would she think? What would she do? Would she at least try to like Yerba Buena? Would she see the potential of being the one who got to shape the new land? He was banking heavily on her tenacity in that regard. But that tenacity was a two-edged sword and he'd been cut by it today at Stewart's. She'd had the temerity to argue with him in public.

Ben watched her chatting with the girls, trying to engage them in conversation. His daughters had not been the easiest of children today. They'd been polite but cool toward her and at times he'd thought he detected an effort to make Moira's job of shopping more difficult than it needed to be. She handled it admirably, though. She'd been undaunted by that coolness. Perhaps because she was uniquely situated through her own experiences of loss to understand how the girls might feel. That had certainly recommended her to him.

He was counting on that experience to help his daughters navigate this new family he was forming for them, this mother he was giving them. *She'll never be Sarah,* the voice of doubt, which sounded an awful lot like his mother, whispered. No. She would not be Sarah. She would be something different and he hoped it would be enough.

He'd never thought of his children as difficult before, but then there was another divide as well. He'd not spent much time with them over the last three years, preferring instead to let his mother handle the raising of them while he devoted himself to his classes at West Point. It was a convenient excuse to say he knew nothing of raising two girls, that his mother was eminently better suited to the task. He'd visited on the weekends. It had been less painful that way, easier to bury his grief or ignore it. He could escape the girls' grief as well. But it also meant ignoring being a father, being a family, and ignoring promises he'd made to his wife—to Sarah—in their final moments together. Going to California was a chance to make good on those promises. He'd once loved being a father and being a family. He wanted to love those things again without the hurt that currently dimmed his joy in them.

The tea came; the pots and cups, the hot chocolate for the girls and the tall tiered tray for the table center. There was the usual flurry of activity as everyone filled their plates with delicacies from the tray. "Lizzie, sip carefully, it is hot. You don't want to burn your tongue," Maggie instructed, taking a tentative taste of her own drink. She'd done that all day—instructing Lizzie, speaking for Lizzie. When had Maggie become a…a what? A little mother? A replica of her grandmother, always instructing, always—dare he say it? Nagging?

"If it is too hot, Lizzie, we can pour a bit of cream in to cool it off," Moira adroitly intervened, adding a splash to the little girl's drink. "Try it now."

"Mmm, this is good," Lizzie pronounced with an excited smile on her face. "I could drink this every day. Is there hot chocolate where we're going, Father?" Lizzie turned her brown eyes his way and his heart began to crumble at the sight of her sweet oval face, so like her mother's. Lizzie was the very spit of Sarah, energetic interest lighting up her face, trusting in him to keep her safe no matter what happened, no matter where they went. Only he hadn't been able to do that. He'd not kept Sarah safe. The old guilt threatened to rise up, right here in the middle of Mrs. Partridge's tearoom for ladies, arguably the safest place on Broadway.

"Don't be a goose, Lizzie," Maggie cut in rather sharply before he could answer. "There's *nothing* where we're going." The derision in her tone was her grandmother talking. His mother had been rankly against his making the journey to California and definitely dead set against his taking the girls.

Ben gave his daughter a stern look. "Margaret, California is a chance for us to build a new world." They'd been over this before. There'd been an ugly scene the night he'd told them in June of the trip to California.

"I like the world I have right here. We can stay with Grandmother," Maggie persisted in what was becoming an annoyingly too common show of disobedience and back talk.

To his surprise, Moira leaped into the breach before he was forced to take disciplinary measures. "Think of the new world that awaits you, Maggie. I think it's exciting to go somewhere few Americans have ever been. I don't know much about Yerba Buena, but I'm told there's a harbor and ships from all over the world sail there. Just think of the people we could meet and the beautiful things they might bring from far-off places."

"Someday, Yerba Buena will be a great city," Ben

jumped in before Moira could paint a falsely rosy picture of Yerba Buena. While it was true that it was an "international harbor" in many ways, it was also untamed. "Jonathan Stevenson, who is sponsoring the regiment, believes it can become the New York of the West Coast." That would be years in the making. Frontiers didn't become towns overnight but the answer seemed to redirect Maggie. This was why he needed Moira. His mother was strict with the girls in some ways but lenient in others and the idea of staying behind was one his mother had put into their heads with repeated regularity ever since he'd proposed the trip.

"It's been decided that you'll come with me. California is too far. We would be separated for years," Ben patiently reminded his daughter with a smile. There were other reasons, too, as to why he would not contemplate a years-long separation. He'd not been there when Sarah had needed him. How could he keep the girls safe if they were a continent away from him?

"Tell us more about California and the men in your regiment," Moira interjected, trying to keep Maggie's spirits up. "I know very little of the project."

Ben took the none-too-subtle conversational offering and eased into the subject. "The regiment is to fill two purposes. First, we're to help fight the war against Mexico wherever we are needed. Some of the companies will go to the Baja area at the southern tip of California. Others may go a little further north to the fort at Monterey. My company, H Company, is slated to stay at the Presidio at Yerba Buena.

"Secondly, no one expects the war to last much longer and when it is over, the United States will be in charge of a very large piece of land. Our regiment is expected to stay and settle it." He had political misgivings over the reasons the United States wanted the land and the potential repercussions of expansion, but he needed this chance and this change. Besides, he reasoned, if he was truly worried about the consequences of settling, he would be better positioned to make those arguments there than from the distance of New England.

He glanced between the girls, Lizzie looking excited, Maggie still looking sullen. Then, he allowed himself to look across the table at Moira. She was smiling and looking utterly delightful in a citified sort of way. She was stunningly beautiful in her black-and-white plaid gown, her hair done up, not a shiny curl out of place, her gray eyes lively and intelligent. He'd tried to parse out how many times he looked at her today, in order to prevent staring, and to prevent being overwhelmed by her loveliness. Physical beauty was a fleeting treasure and often a false one. Beauty could be bought, cultivated, with things like satin ribbons and dancing slippers, but that didn't mean it was without power. He did not wish to be lured by it.

"Most of the men in the regiment are mechanics of various kinds. They all have a skill or a trade they can ply in California. They are bringing the tools of their trades with them. We will need all their skill once the war is over. California will need blacksmiths and farmers, and coopers, all sorts. It will need their education, too. Many of the men in my regiment are men of letters as well as a craft." Ben felt himself smile as he talked, the thrill of taming a new land humming through him. There would be work aplenty. He'd be busy sunrise to sunset, carving out a new life. Busy enough to even forget the old one and the pain that had gone with it.

"Are there many families coming as well?" Moira asked over the rim of her teacup.

"No, nor many wives. Most of the men recruited are young and unmarried." It was hoped that they might marry the Spanish settlers there and use those alliances to establish and maintain the peace. And American women would follow, eventually, once the city was built. "There are the officers' wiveson the other ships , though. You won't be entirely without female company," he added in assurance.

They'd nearly finished their tea when a small group of ladies approached the table, Mrs. Bostwick, his hostess from the house party, at their head. He sensed Moira stiffen, her posture a bit straighter, her gaze guarded and suspecting. Ben felt himself go on the defensive on her behalf. This was the woman who had exiled his soon-to-be wife from the house party.

"Major Sheffield, it is you!" Mrs. Bostwick gushed as he rose to greet them.

"And Miss Blackthorne as well." Ben gestured to Moira, forcing Mrs. Bostwick to acknowledge his fiancée. He would not allow this busybody of a woman to slight his fiancée in public.

Mrs. Bostwick gave Moira a quick, curt nod. "Miss Blackthorne, out for tea just a day before your marriage? I can't imagine having time for such leisure with the rush of the wedding." She smiled coyly but Ben did not miss the jab she was taking at the haste behind their marriage. He could fairly feel Moira bristling. Even on short acquaintance, he knew Moira would not hesitate to take a few jabs of her own at Mrs. Bostwick and *that* he could not permit, not for Moira's sake, his sake or for his girls.

"The military is a hard taskmaster, Mrs. Bostwick. The regiment ships out on the twenty-sixth. We have little say in the matter. We wed on military time." He glanced at Moira and managed a little smile meant to convey the sentiments of a bridegroom. "Otherwise, my bride would have a proper courtship. As it is, she'll have to settle for a proper wedding. The family has it all well in hand. Haste or not, rest assured Gemma Blackthorne will have Grace Church turned out to its best tomorrow. I assume you'll be there to wish us well?"

There were a few more moments of small talk and when it became apparent he was not going to order more chairs so that Mrs. Bostwick and friends could join them, Mrs. Bostwick moved on. "You dispatched her quite neatly," Moira said as he sat back down. A grudging sense of achievement filled him at her words. He had pleased her, and he found that pleased him in some small degree. It was a much more satisfactory feeling than the sense that he'd disappointed her in the department store. He wasn't entirely sure the disappointment had been about the ribbons or about something larger.

"I will not allow the Mrs. Bostwicks of the world to cast a shadow over you or our wedding." He looked around the table and at the demolished tea tray. "Besides, it's time we were getting home. Tomorrow will be a long day and the day after that even longer." He came around the table to Moira's chair and pulled it out. She smelled like vanilla and autumn. He breathed it in and allowed himself to think for fraction of a second how wonderful it was to smell a woman again.

"Thank you," Moira said for his ears alone as she rose. In that moment, in the briefest of flickers, something akin to hope stirred, that perhaps, in time, this marriage might be enough for his girls, and for him, that there might be room for friendship, which was, of course, all he could allow there to be.

Chapter Five

September 24, 1846

She was going to be late for her own wedding! That had not been her intention when she'd left this morning. But good intentions being what they were, she was now rushing into the house and up the stairs to find a worried Gemma waiting in her room. "There you are! Where have you been?"

"Stewart's, one last errand." Moira brandished the small, brown-paper-wrapped package in one hand as proof before tucking it into the bag that would accompany her to the hotel after the wedding festivities.

Not just *the* wedding. *Her* wedding. An event that was scheduled to take place in just under an hour. Even with the nearness of the event approaching, it still bore trappings of the surreal. The last few days had been a blur of activity; shopping and pack-

ing, then more shopping and more packing. She and
Gemma had worked late into the evening last night
long after the major and his daughters had left. She'd
been busy, the activities serving to obscure where
it all led; to the altar, facing a man she barely knew
and joining her life, her *fate*, to his.

It had not seemed real last night when she'd closed
the final trunk and sent it off to the ship with the
others. Nor had it seemed possible when she'd lain
down to sleep that it was the last night she'd go to
bed in her childhood room.

"What are you thinking, Moira? You seem lost,"
Gemma asked, moving around the room, laying out
clean underthings and petticoats.

"I'm wondering if this is how Henry VIII's
wives felt the morning of their executions, as if they
wouldn't really happen, that it was all some kind of
play and soon it would be over and real life would
start again."

Gemma laughed and came to her, taking her
hands. Together, they sat on the edge of her bed.
"This is a wedding, not an execution. Besides, Henry
only beheaded two of them."

Moira laughed in spite of herself. "That does not
make it better, Gem." She would miss her brother's wife, this lovely woman who had befriended her
as a sister even when the young girl she'd been—
a girl who'd been resentful of her brother's marriage—hadn't always deserved it. "It is a beheading
of sorts, though," Moira persisted with her rather
morbid theme. "Today, I am cut off from my old life,

the minute I become Mrs. Sheffield." Not even her name would be the same. By noon, Moira Blackthorne would no longer legally exist. Who would she be then?

"Endings are also beginnings, my dear. You have a wondrous adventure awaiting you." Gemma insisted. "You are not cut off from your old life. We'll write letters. I'll send you all the latest news and you'll likely be back for a visit in five years when Margaret comes of age. The Sheffield roots are here, after all, and Grandmother Sheffield will want a brilliant match for her granddaughter."

"Grandmother Sheffield? Are we all friends now? 'Grandmother Sheffield' didn't seem to approve of me yesterday." Moira wrinkled her brow, trying to follow Gemma's conversation. Why would Maggie come back for a debut? Only New York society bothered with such things.

"You know how it is, Moira. Everyone in New York knows everyone. How do you think the major got an invitation to Mrs. Bostwick's house party to start with? His mother's brother is a business acquaintance of Mrs. Bostwick's father in-law, who was more than eager to curry favor in that direction. When the major told his mother he wanted to remarry, it was the matter of a few notes and poof!" Gemma snapped her fingers. "An invitation appears to a party guaranteed to offer a display of New York's finest girls from the best families for the major to choose from."

"How did you learn all of this?" Moira found

Gemma's recitation momentarily distracting as she tried to delve into the layers of connections her sister-in-law presented. Perhaps Gemma was right and she did need to pay better attention to society. Too late for that now, though.

Gemma tossed her a smug smile. "I learned it quite simply over tea with Grandmother Sheffield. You see, your major isn't a nobody. He has connections if he ever wanted to use them." Moira wasn't sure he was "her" major but the comment did offer clarity to Maggie's comment over tea about wanting to stay with her grandmother. "The major's uncle will be at the wedding," Gemma offered a cryptic smile meant to tease her. "Edgar Franks lives in town."

"Edgar Franks?" The Produce King of Manhattan. Moira gaped, pieces falling into place from her conversation with the major earlier. Of course he'd want to go into greengrocery with Edgar Franks as his uncle. No wonder he'd spent so much time at the house party with the man. They were relations and potentially future business associates.

"The very same. He has a lovely home on Bleeker Street, although I hear he's building a new one just off Park Avenue." Gemma smiled softly and patted her hand. "There, you see? We aren't marrying you off to a stranger. Brandon had the major vetted quite thoroughly." Perhaps the major had her vetted as thoroughly.

Her sister in-law meant the words to be comforting and they might have been if they hadn't triggered a suspicion. Had the major not been completely honest with her about his need for a wife and why he'd chosen her? Not just for his children but for his business? A greengrocer in San Francisco would need shipping access. Who better to marry than a shipping magnate's sister?

Before she could follow up, a maid entered with the oyster silk and seed pearl wedding gown laid reverently across her outstretched arms. The gown had belonged to Moira's mother. What had seemed remotely surreal suddenly became concrete at the sight of the gown, a very real symbol of what this day was heading toward. Moira froze. "I can't do it, Gemma. You know more about my husband than I do."

"You have your whole life to get to know him," Gemma assured her with a squeeze of her hands as they rose. "Love will come, Moira. Just as it did for me and your brother. We were not in love on our wedding day. I daresay not many couples are. But marriage will be what you choose to make it." Gemma turned her over to the maid with an admonition for haste as the maid helped her out of her clothes and into her bridal finery: fresh petticoats, a chemise threaded with a pretty pink ribbon, silk stockings and a corset laced tight.

At last, she stepped into the oyster silk gown that had belonged to her mother another lifetime ago. If she breathed in carefully, she could still catch the faintest scent of her mother's lavender. It calmed her, comforted her.

Moira turned slowly to face herself in the long pier glass, Gemma gasping softly behind her. What would her mother think of today? Of her? Of this marriage? Would she be ashamed of her reckless daughter? Embarrassed by the circumstances that had led to this wedding? *Love keeps no record of wrongs.* It was one of her mother's favorite verses and floated through her head now as she smoothed the silk skirts. She spoke over her shoulder to Gemma, "Mother would let me try this dress on once or twice when I was growing up." The last time had been when she was nine. The bodice had sagged and the skirts had been too long. "I always felt like a princess."

"And today you are one." Gemma led her to the dressing table. "We'll have to hurry with your hair." They were doing their best for her, Moira realized. If she didn't like the situation she found herself in today, she had only herself to blame. She'd been warned to take care and she'd not listened. Now, at last, her brother had despaired of her or of himself being able to protect her.

The maid had just finished the final touches on her coiffure when there was a rap at her door. "That will be Brandon. He'll want a moment with you." Gemma answered the door and slipped out with the maid to give them privacy.

Moira rose on shaky legs to greet her brother. She held out her skirts for inspection and said in a breathy voice that betrayed her nerves, "Well, how do I look?"

Brandon was silent for a moment, his eyes sheened with emotion. "Beautiful. Like a bride." He came to her then and kissed her cheek with brotherly affection. "I brought you these." He held out a square blue velvet box and opened the lid.

"Mother's pearls," Moira gasped. "Oh, I couldn't. They should go to your wife, to Gemma."

Brandon shook his head. "No, they are meant to be yours on your wedding day." He took them from the box and stepped behind her, fastening them about her neck.

Moira fingered them, guilt creeping in. "They were meant for a real wedding, not one like this."

"This *is* a real wedding, Moira." Brandon stepped back to admire her. "You look like her, you know."

"But I'm not like her, not in the ways that count," Moira insisted. "I'm not patient, I'm not good, not like she was."

Brandon chuckled. "Give yourself time. You hardly know yourself. Who knows what you'll discover. I have faith in you, Moira. And in Major Sheffield. He is a good man. I wouldn't have let you go if I didn't think the arrangement had potential."

"I know." She did understand that much at least. . She might know very little about him. He was stern and strict with his daughters, but he was loving, too. He'd stood, quite literally, between her and Mrs. Bostwick yesterday. "Still, Bran, five years is a long time. Little Ethan will be six before I see him again." She'd not been away from Brandon or home for any significant period of time, certainly not for five years. So much would happen, they would have lives and experiences without her. "Ethan will forget me." What she really meant was that they might all forget her.

"I won't allow it." Brandon gave her a smile and reached for the veil of antique lace, taking it from the bed. He settled it on her head with a laugh at his clumsy efforts. "You'd better do it and then we need to go."

"A prayer before we go?" She was desperate to delay this very departure, the first of many she'd be making today and tomorrow, all of them final in their own ways. "Do the one you used to say right after Mother and Father died and I was scared."

Brandon smiled. "You haven't been scared a day in your life, but I'll say it anyway." They bent their foreheads together, their hands gripping one another in the old ritual. When had they stopped this, she wondered, letting the ritual soothe her even if she believed the words fell on holy deaf ears.

"Dear Lord, look down on this little family and wrap it in the shield of Your protection." This was how it always began. Her brother's words brought calm as he continued, these words new. "Be with Moira as she begins a new life, bring her wisdom and peace. Open her heart to the possibilities that lay before her. Be with her husband, grant him patience and forgiveness. In Your name we pray, amen."

Moira looked up, emotion riding her hard. It would be better to laugh than to cry. "Patience and forgiveness? Do you think my husband will need such things?" she teased lightly.

Brandon checked his pocket watch. "He'll need

them both quite immediately given that we're late."
He held the door for her and she stepped out into the
hall without a backward glance. Time had run out
on her childhood.

Major Benjamin Sheffield was the sort of man
who liked punctuality. He required it of himself and
expected it in others, although it had not always been
that way in his youth. Still, he'd been on time for his
first marriage and he'd been on time for his second.
He could not say the same for his bride. She was late
by a quarter of an hour and counting, which left him
to face down a squirming gaggle of guests at Grace
Church with an expression of placid equanimity.

Heads swiveled at every sound to the solid oak
doors at the rear of the chapel and then back to him;
how was he responding to the late arrival? Was he
worried? Did he think the reckless Moira Blackthorne
had jilted him at the altar? He could read the naked
speculation in their faces and he was doubly glad he
was taking the little spitfire away from all this.

Mrs. Bostwick, matronly hypocrite that she was,
sat down front in pride of place, beaming over the
fact that she'd come across the major and Miss Blackthorne taking tea with the girls yesterday. Yesterday,
of all things! Could you believe it? To think that
she'd been the one to play matchmaker at her house
party. And she had, although not in the way one
might think. It had been her attitude toward Moira
Blackthorne that had decided him. What was it she'd
said? That girls like Moira grew up to be a disgrace

to their families? That she was too high spirited to ever be tamed now? Ruin was just a scandal away.

Her warning had only made him look more closely at the dark-haired minx who'd dared Edward Brant. He couldn't say he liked what he saw—he hardly knew the young woman —but he could empathize with it. He'd been much the same in his youth; reckless, overconfident. The military had been the making of him, giving him the structure and direction he needed to cross the threshold into adulthood. He'd had the military, but what did a someone like Moira have? There was no military for her. There was only marriage and the hopes of a husband who might polish that diamond in the rough. He could be that for her, if she would let him.

The doors at the back of the church were pulled open at last, and heads swiveled one final time amid a rustle of fabric and movement. The quartet engaged for the ceremony began to play something soft and stately, he couldn't say what it was. All of his attention was riveted on the figure who came through the door: Moira Blackthorne, escorted by her brother in a beam of autumn late morning sunlight that seemed to follow her down the aisle as if nature had given its blessing to the hasty union even if Mrs. Bostwick had not. She reached him and stood at the front of the church, head held high, defying anyone who dared to point out she was tardy to her own nuptials.

She was dressed in a gown of oyster silk. Gemma had described it to him and the girls the night before and the detail did not do the gown—justice. It was expensively trimmed with yards of Belgium lace that dripped from the bodice and the short, puffed sleeves with seed pearls embroidering the hem. Pearls also adorned the base of her neck and she wore her copious amounts of walnut-dark hair in a soft twist beneath her veil. She looked like a wood nymph, fresh and beautiful, with a bit of mischief in her gray eyes when they caught his—and bravery, too. He did not overlook that. They were both being brave today. Her brother placed her hand in his and his heart began to pound. Not from love or lust or any other bridegroom-ly sentiment. Worry was having one last go at him.

Had he made the right decision in betting on her tenacity? Had he chosen wisely? For the task at hand? For his daughters?

It was not the first time such thoughts had come to him. He'd behaved somewhat rashly in selecting her—a trait unusual for him—but he consoled himself that time had not been on his side. He'd had to choose one of them. Why not her? Surely, her tenacity was better than the others' timidity. And yet she was the sister of a wealthy shipping magnate. What did she know of rough living? She wore a gown today that would not last in Yerba Buena. Silk had no place there. The gown was like those satin ribbons the girls had fawned over. Her words came back to him: *Perhaps that's the very reason for them, something beautiful amid the dreariness.*

He gave her and her brother a solemn nod and fixed a picture of her in his mind against the time to come. She would not dress like this in the West. Would she mind that so very much? Did she realize? Perhaps she did not. Doubts and worry swirled hard in his mind. Sarah had realized. She'd known exactly what it meant to marry him, the kind of life she would have as a young officer's wife, either waiting at home or following wherever he went. She'd chosen the latter, which had turned out to be in the wilds of the Michigan Territory, . An isolated but tame enough post. Then the children had come and they'd gone to West Point for his professorship, aspiring to a stable life at the academy.

His heart had pounded on that first wedding day, too, but for different reasons. He'd married for love that day, not convenience. He'd waited and worked for that moment all his life it seemed. Marrying Sarah had been the deliberate trajectory of his adolescence and early adulthood. He'd courted her with a young man's ardor for three years before earning her father's approval. Whereas, he'd barely spent half an hour with Miss Blackthorne before marriage had been decided. Now, they were facing a lifetime together. They were either both very brave indeed or very foolhardy.

The reverend intoned the opening words of the ceremony. *Dearly beloved, we are gathered here today to join this man and this woman in the bonds of holy matrimony...* Ben knew them by heart. He remembered how he'd longed to hear those words. His wedding day had been the happiest day of his life until his daughters were born. Today was nothing like that, never mind that Gemma Blackthorne had worked miracles in four days; there was a quartet, white roses, satin ribbon garland looped between the pews and a church crowded with guests, many of whom were friends of the Blackthornes.

One would never guess the wedding had been hastily decided upon. There would be a breakfast to follow, hosted by her brother at the elegant Blackthorne brownstone on West Fourteenth. Sarah and he had not had a lavish wedding breakfast, just a meal with their families at a local inn with his comrades in arms. Even so, the day had been one of the grandest of his life, proof that money didn't buy happiness. Love did.

No, despite today's elegant trappings and the beautiful bride beside him at the altar, Ben could not equate the two weddings. One he had worked for, yearned for and one he was grasping at in haste, desperate to provide a mother for his girls. One was a match made in love, the other made out of practical need where love wasn't a consideration. Sarah had broken his heart when she died. He didn't want to travel that road again, didn't want to feel like that again, didn't want to give another the power to hurt him like that again.

"Do you, Benjamin Michael Sheffield, take Moira Catherine Blackthorne to be your lawfully wedded wife?" Ben let the words wash over him; *to have and to hold from this day forward, for better, for worse, for richer, for poorer, in sickness and in health, to love and to cherish, till death us do part?* He was not twenty-one anymore, the words no longer a romantic fancy. He'd lived this promise. Failed in this promise once before. If not for the girls, he'd not thought to make these pledges again, and yet here he was.

"I do." His voice filled Grace Church as if it were the parade grounds on Governor's Island, and his gaze did not waver from hers, letting her see that he meant his promise. He did not take this lightly. Her protection would be his duty in exchange for her duty: to raise his girls, to care for his home. She, in turn, would have a chance to escape, a chance to build a new life less regulated by social rules designed to strangle her.

The vows repeated for her and he felt her hand give the slightest tremble in his. He ran his thumbs over her knuckles in support. Good, she had some sense, then, this reckless bride he'd taken. She knew enough to at least be reverent of the promise she was making. There could be no turning back for either of them.

There were rings and a final prayer, then the admonition that he may kiss the bride. It was a public kiss, warm lips pressed against one another, and some regret stirred in him that their first intimacy was to be conducted before an audience. Perhaps he should have stayed in Manhattan instead of haring back to his men and duty the night before the girls arrived. It would have given them time to become better acquainted even just a fraction more.

The reverend introduced the couple to the congregation: Major and Mrs. Sheffield. Ben took her arm through his and led his new wife down the aisle. There was no going back. For better or for worse started right now.

Chapter Six

They were alone for the first time since the proposal, a situation magnified by the silent opulence of the Park Hotel's best suite, a gift from the major's uncle. "One final night of luxury," the major said at last as he helped her with her wrap and draped it across the back of the white sofa.

It was one last night of many things, Moira thought, making a tour of the room to offset her nervous energy. It was a last night in the city she'd grown up in, a last night near her family. A last night on land for six months. A last night in the life she knew, and a first night with her new husband, not that anything would come of it as traditional wedding nights went. Still, being alone with this man, *her husband*, for the first time brought its own anxious brand of excitement. Better to focus on the room.

It was a pretty suite. Everything in the main salon was white: the sofa, the chairs, the long filmy cur-

tains that ornamented the French doors leading out
to the balcony and the view beyond. White for the
wedding, white for their marriage, although his uncle
couldn't have known that. The only color in the room
was the dark red roses blooming from a vase on the
sideboard and her husband in the dark coat and trousers of his dress uniform.

Moira watched the major as he made his way to
the polished sideboard with its roses, cut crystal decanter and two matched tumblers. He'd been a veritable pillar of resolution and strength through the
service and the wedding breakfast, exuding confidence, control and command. His hand had never left
the small of her back as they'd greeted the guests.
He'd given the appearance of being a well-satisfied
bridegroom, one who'd looked forward to this day
with pleased relish. One would not have guessed
he'd proposed only four days ago, pushed to it by an
encroaching deadline and the need to take a mother
to California for his daughters. Even now, with the
distractions of the day removed, leaving them both
exposed to the consequences of their haste—being
alone with a virtual stranger—he was still in command. If he shared any of the nerves racing through
her, he gave no sign of them. Then again, he commanded men. How intimidating could one woman
be?

"Cider?" he asked, holding up the amber-filled decanter before pouring a drink for each of them. She
took the tumbler and took a seat on the sofa, silence
engulfing them once more now that the room had

been toured and beverages poured. What did one say to a man they hardly knew? Perhaps this was why she'd insisted they linger at the wedding breakfast until it was nearly unseemly to remain any longer. The last four days she'd been surrounded by people and busyness. There'd been no time to think, only to do, and there'd been a lot to do. Even this morning had been a whirlwind right up to the altar. The ceremony had been a surreal blur, the wedding breakfast a collage of faces, hugs, handshakes and well-wishes, some more genuine than others.

The festivities had been heavily attended despite the short notice. Her brother and Gemma had made good on their promise to give her a wedding to be proud of. The high society of New York had turned out for her sendoff, some because they were friends, but some had come to gloat. When the shiny veneer of a whirlwind romance wore off, the plain truth remained and the Mrs. Bostwicks of society would not overlook it: She was off to rugged parts and a life that was viewed as a definite comedown from the mansions of Manhattan no matter how attractive her husband. She was marrying down and she was lucky to have married at all before some scandal of her making in the near-off future destroyed her family's reputation. If people wanted to gossip about her hasty marriage, she trusted Brandon to put the gossip down. Not that she cared for her sake. By the time those rumors made the rounds, she'd be far from shore. Those rumors could not touch her.

"Will you miss all of this terribly?" The major

waved his glass to indicate the suite as he took a seat across from her in the wing-backed chair.

"Probably on occasion." Moira met his question with directness. It wasn't the obvious luxuries she was worried about living without, things like crystal decanters and satin gowns sewn with seed pearls. It was the unseen luxury, privileges she wasn't even aware of populating her day like the ease of moving from event to event. When she had plans, baths were drawn, gowns laid out before she even gave the order. Her clothes were always laundered and pressed, ready for her at any given moment. Carriages waiting.

Her husband gave a short chuckle at her honesty. "Only on occasion?"

"There are definitely things I won't miss," Moira added. "I prefer to focus on that." She could see that surprised him.

"Like what?" he asked, his gaze resting on her face in contemplation as he sipped his cider—his drink of choice she noted.

"All of society's rules. I've never had much use for all those artificial standards about how to live. Takes all the fun out of it."

Her words teased a smile from him, a real smile, not the polite one he'd offered to the guests. This smile softened the commanding lines of his jaw and took ten years off him. He should try that more often, Moira thought. He raised his glass. "To all that is to be gained, then."

"You prefer cider." Moira groped for something

to say after they drank their cider toast. "Are you a temperance man?"

"Not primarily. Although I am familiar with Lyman Beecher's teachings on the subject, one can hardly live in New England and not be." He gave a wry smile. "I've seen alcohol ruin plenty of good soldiers and sailors. I prefer to keep my wits clear at all times. I don't impose a no-drinking policy on my men, but I do hope to inspire them to the same choice by leading through example."

"Have you always been a soldier?" Moira eagerly picked up the conversational offering. Surely, this topic would keep them busy until she could decently retire to her bedchamber. Most of the men she knew relished any opportunity to talk about themselves, and what better chance would she have to get to know more about her husband? Tomorrow they would be surrounded by people again and the girls. Privacy would become a rare commodity. The aloneness of tonight was both a blessing and a curse in the offering of this time together.

He studied his glass, and for a moment she thought she'd lost him. He seemed to go from her, from this room, as if the liquid in his glass conjured up other memories of another time and place. He looked at her, his blue eyes steady. "Yes, I've always wanted to be a soldier. The structure and the order of the military, the comradeship of living in community with others who appreciated the same, appealed to me as did the idea of travel and adventure. I wanted to be an officer, to lead men in the great historical tradition of Darius and Alexander, Hannibal and Leonidas. I was fortunate enough through my uncle's connections to study at West Point, although I daresay he'd have preferred a different path for me."

"Did he want you to go into greengrocery with him?" Moira inquired with a little laugh. She could not picture her straight-backed, broad-shouldered husband as a city's greengrocer. A narrow store on a crowded street seemed, somehow, too small for him. A man his size was meant for wide-open spaces and perhaps the adventure he'd alluded to, although the stern man who'd shopped with her yesterday and proposed to her two days prior had not struck her as an adventurer. That man was a practical man. Yet, who else but an adventurer would find the appeal in the journey to California? Further proof that Major Benjamin Sheffield was more than he seemed.

"My uncle was very keen on it," he replied. "He and my aunt have no children of their own. Fortunately, I have another cousin who feels called to greengrocery." He gave a half laugh.

"Lucas Fielding," Moira supplied. "I met him today." He was as rich as Croesus; dressed like it, too, with a gold ring on each finger.

"Ah, yes, Lucas." There was a hint of censure in his tone. He would not disparage his cousin but neither did she sense there was deep feeling between them. Or perhaps the censure was for himself? Remorse perhaps over a path not chosen?

"Do you regret your decision? You could have made a fortune." Moira gave him a quizzing glance.

"Or perhaps your fortune is yet to be made in California?"

The question caught him off guard. For a moment he'd simply stared at her. "You are a bold one. I thought well-bred young women didn't talk about money."

"Such young ladies often find themselves unpleasantly surprised because they didn't ask," Moira answered swiftly, letting her tongue get ahead of her thoughts. Belatedly, she wondered what he would make of her boldness. Surely, he wouldn't be startled by it. He'd said her boldness appealed to him, but perhaps not when it was turned his direction as it had been yesterday over hair ribbons and just now.

His eyes narrowed as if he understood she was testing him in his response, a test that might very well set the tone for how such conversations would be handled throughout their marriage. "It's to be hoped such young ladies have male family members to ask on their behalf as your brother did." As he had yesterday, he tried to subdue her bold comment with a subtle reminder, and like yesterday, her active mind ran roughshod over such subtlety.

"I'd rather be able to take care of myself instead of relying on someone else to do it for me."

"I expect you would," he responded dryly. Too late, Moira saw the trap. The test wasn't just for him. He'd been testing her, too. What had begun as a polite question about her husband's career had become an argument about finances and a woman's place in the home. She wasn't even out of her wedding dress yet and she'd managed to politicize a simple conversation. Was he regretting his decision already? Was this boldness of hers more than he'd bargained for, after all? She could not divine an answer from his posture. She didn't want him to regret it, she wanted him to understand it, and accept it. Perhaps not all at once, but in time.

Moira picked up the previous strand of conversation, the less contentious one. "Tell me about after West Point. Did you get your adventure?"

He shook his head. "It turned out to not be terribly adventurous. I was posted to Fort Brady in Sault Ste. Marie on the American-Canadian border in the Michigan territory. The fort is meant to protect against British incursions but we saw little more action than managing smugglers. Even so, once Maggie was born, a wilderness fort was no place to raise a baby."

Although he might have liked it to have been. She detected a twist of wistfulness beneath his words. Despite downplaying the excitement of the wilderness fort, he'd not been ready to give it up. Yet he had given it up to be a father, a family man. A soldier and a father, two roles that demanded sacrifice combined in one man. "So you returned to West Point?" Moira prompted, intrigued by how his story ended. She did wish he was a bit more forthcoming. Getting him to elaborate was akin to pulling teeth.

He looked into his glass, remembering again. "During my studies, I'd always enjoyed languages and military history as a cadet. When the post became available, it seemed as if the Hand of Providence had moved in my direction. I've enjoyed teaching."

"But now you'll have California," Moira offered. It would be his redemption, a chance to get back what he'd given up to be a family man. Now, he could combine the adventurer with the father, old dreams with new. Beneath the controlled exterior he showed the world was a man who'd waited thirteen years to return to those dreams. Not unlike her. It would be thirteen years this spring since her parents had died. Between then and now had been thirteen years of waiting; waiting to come alive again, waiting for her heart to heal, and realizing she might be waiting forever.

"You will have California, too." He held her gaze steady with his own. They would have a new life, a new land and whatever they made of that chance between them. A moment of accord rippled, warm with feeling, and when it passed, Moira felt they might be a little less a pair of strangers to one another.

"Tell me about the men." His new wife was a font of questions. Were the questions from curiosity? Nerves? A combination of both perhaps? Daylight was fading from the salon.

Ben took the opportunity to move about the room, lighting the lamps and refilling their tumblers. It had been dark when he'd risen this morning and it was dark again, testimony that the long day was coming full circle. His bride had born up admirably and still apparently had the temerity to argue over women's financial rights with him. What an odd wedding day this was and an odder night still in contrast with his first one. Suffice it to say, he'd not spent his first wedding night discussing his troops. "The men are coming along," he offered carefully. He didn't want to dismay her.

"The *Herald* says the men are of the highest caliber and that the mission's success is guaranteed." She slanted a coy look over the rim of her glass. Was she daring him to argue with her?

"The *Herald* has been a great supporter of Colonel Stevenson's venture, perhaps even to the point of slight exaggeration," he acceded. "Whereas the *Tribune* has overexaggerated the contrary. We are neither an assembly of heroes nor a rabble of malcontents. But we are in truth, for better or worse, volunteers." He'd spent most of August teaching the untrained men to drill, to conform to the strict custom of the army. Only through organization and uniform adherence to order could a large body function with any success. There'd been days when he'd despaired of achieving the most basic of tasks with them. Then, there had been the political trouble attempting to waylay Stevenson's personal departure with the troops. He would be more than relieved when the ships left the harbor.

"Are you a volunteer as well?" Moira asked perceptively, a lovely smile twitching at her mouth, giving the impression that she was teasing him.

"Yes, in a strict sense, I am. Most of the officers

on this mission are field officers from West Point, professors like myself." Men like him who'd decided now was the time to remake their lives. Where better to do that than in a place so far from home not even the ghosts of the past could follow. "President Polk wanted a military who could serve dual purpose as both soldiers and settlers. My knowledge of Spanish will be helpful after the war, and, of course, the fort will need soldiers. But it will also need blacksmiths, farriers, farmers, coopers and millers. Many of these new recruits have packed their tools beside their weapons. As for my regiment, a new territory will need people with skills of all sorts. My men were selected not so much for their fighting skills as for their educational skills, reading, writing, learning. Along with farmers we will need journalists." The thought of it brought a smile. There would be a literal hammering of swords into plowshares in a very short time. The war with Mexico wouldn't last much longer.

His bride discreetly stifled a yawn behind her hand and he realized he must have been going on. The hours had fled. He rose. "It will be an early morning and a long day. We should retire. I'll show you to your chamber," he added with the intention to clarify that he didn't intend to break his word.

There were two bedrooms, one on each side of the salon, each equipped with an enormous, comfortable bed. He saw her to the one on the right and took a look around, ascertaining she had all she needed. Her gown for the morning was already hung up. Her bag was on the bench at the foot of the bed and her nightgown had been laid out by the maid who'd seen to her bag. His gaze lingered there on the fine-linen night-rail embroidered with pink flowers and tiny green leaves at the bodice. It seemed the height of intimacy to see such a personal item. Better to think of her as she was now, her dark hair decorously piled on her head, the demure lines of the heavy satin of her wedding gown, the fall of her full skirts.

Her wedding gown! The thought hit him all at once. She'd never be able to get out of that feminine confection on her own and it was too late to call for a maid. There was nothing for it. A gentleman wouldn't leave her to struggle alone, or worse, force her to conclude on her own that she needed help and be required to seek him out in his own room. "It's been a while since I've played the lady's maid, but I seem to recall gowns require extra hands. Shall I render my services before I retire for the night?"

Chapter Seven

She had to accept. She'd never get out of the dress on her own and they both knew it. The question was a formality, a warning, a polite anticipation of her needs. But knowing that didn't stop the hot flush that crept up her cheeks at the thought of being undressed. "Help would be wonderful, thank you."

Moira drew a breath and gave him her back, trying to appear unaffected by the offer. This was one of many practical intimacies that could not be avoided in the close quarters and shared spaces of daily living.

He made short work of the buttons and she felt the gown grow slack about her. Moira clutched the satin to her, an involuntary act of modesty made from reflex as his hands dealt with the petticoat tapes and they slid to the ground at her feet beneath the gown, hidden from view.

Without warning, he stepped back, the space between them suddenly colder. She'd not realized the warmth his presence had supplied. Nor could she have anticipated the sense of loss when his touch was gone. Her stays were loose. His hands would come no closer. There was no need to help her with her chemise. That could be easily managed on her own *and* alone. "I'm sure you can take things from here," he offered congenially.

She turned to face him, struggling for something to say. "Well, good night, then. The morning will be here before we know it."

One his wry smiles teased at his mouth. "Good night, Moira." He hesitated a moment longer. Moira had the sense he was waiting for something. When it didn't come, he gave her a small bow and departed her chamber, heading to his room across the salon.

Only when he was gone did she realize what he'd wanted. His name. He'd wanted her to say his name. It was a small enough courtesy to offer him after all the courtesies he'd offered her. His every thought, his every action today had been for her benefit.

Even though he knew what this marriage really was, an act of convenience to save her from inevitable scandal—if it wasn't the Bostwick debacle, it would be something sooner or later—and to provide his daughters with a new mother in a strange land.

Even though he'd not have chosen her otherwise.

Even though he had no intention of making this a marriage in truth.

Even though he loved another and loved that other still.

A litany of "even thoughs" ran through Moira's head as she readied herself for bed. The last one resonated the loudest: even though this wedding day must have taken an enormous emotional toll on him. He'd set all that aside for her to create the appearance of an eager bridegroom. And all he'd wanted in return was to hear his name. She would do better tomorrow, Moira vowed. She turned down the lamp beside her bed and whispered quietly into the lonely dark, "Good night, Ben."

September 25, 1846

The *Loo Choo* stood in the harbor, sails flaccid, as Moira watched the last of her things being loaded. The girls stood beside her. This luggage would go straight to their cabin. It was barely noon, but Moira felt as if the day should be ending. She'd been up since dawn. They'd taken an early breakfast at the hotel, then collected Maggie and Lizzie from Bleeker Street.

The farewell with Grandmother Sheffield had been tearful and angsty. Maggie had made one last defiant bid for freedom by refusing to come out of her room. As a result, they'd arrived later than anticipated at the docks, something that had not sat well with the major, who'd immediately disappeared after telling them to stay put, something that had not sat well with *her*.

After an hour of "staying put," Moira was tired and cross. Lizzie was hopping around in excitement, trying to see everything at once and asking questions at full speed. How many people would be on board? Would there be any children to play with? Would there be any storms? What would the food be like? Would they see dolphins? Could they swim in the ocean? Moira was having a hard time keeping an eye on Lizzie and trying to answer her questions while making sure Maggie didn't attempt to slip away. So far, Maggie hadn't moved an inch. She just stood there in an obvious sulk, having not said a word since she'd gotten in the carriage.

Moira wanted to say something to the girl but what? She was in no position to give assurances and she would not begin their relationship with lies. Neither was she in a position to discipline Maggie for her behavior. Not that she wanted to. This was a huge move, an enormous change. It was taking the girls from everything and everyone they knew.

A somberly dressed man approached them, touching his fingers to the brim of his hat. He had a long, striking, stern face with hollowed-out cheeks and sharp dark eyes. "Mrs. Sheffield?" For a moment, Moira forgot that was her now. She was Mrs. Sheffield. "I'm Doctor Reverend John MacVickar. Your husband sent me. Congratulations on your nuptials yesterday." He made her a small bow. "These two lovely ladies must be the major's daughters. I'm pleased to meet you and I've brought you something." He held out a Bible to her and offered the girls two small prayer books. "On Wednesday, I did a sermon for the men before they boarded the ships and we presented them with Bibles. Your husband explained the family was unable to be there. I thought you would enjoy the comfort of a Bible on the voyage, Mrs. Sheffield, and that you and the girls might like to pray before boarding."

She must truly be feeling surly. It was on the tip of her tongue to say "what for?" None of her prayers had been answered this week; not the prayer to stop the wedding, to make the major change his mind. When that didn't work, she'd turned to other desperate prayers. She was married to a stranger and that couldn't be changed, but maybe leaving New York could. God might stir up a storm that prevented the ships from leaving, or to preclude the regiments from leaving at all. God had not seen fit to do that, either. Hence, here she was at the bottom of the gangplank preparing to sail away from the city she'd been raised in.

Revered MacVickar's gaze rested on her face as if he read her thoughts. "A prayer can't hurt. Shall we?" He bowed his head and offered a blessing for safe passage and strong faith on the voyage and for a good life in California. When he concluded, he took the Bible from her and opened it to the back. "There's a place to note your marriage and the names of family members." He showed her. "You can put your name and your husband's here, and the girls' here."

Maggie snorted. "She's not our real mother."

The reverend quelled her with a strong look. "God has seen fit to give you a mother to act in her place.

You are very blessed, child, to have a mother on earth and one in heaven."

"I'd rather be less blessed, then." Maggie's eyes were steely-blue flints. "I liked the one I had." Maggie's defiance was too much like her own, Moira thought. She'd been given such platitudes as the reverend gave Maggie with much the same result. Perhaps she could share with the girl later when they had a moment alone. She knew from experience that trying to get through to an angry adolescent in a public place with said adolescent in a hot temper would not be successful.

The reverend bid them farewell with promises to pray for their safe passage and they were alone again on the docks. Even Lizzie was beginning to tire of waiting when the major returned for them.

"Everything is prepared for you to board," he informed them. He nodded at the prayer books his girls held. "I see the reverend found you. Are you ready?"

Moira bristled. "We have been ready, sir." She met him squarely with her rejoinder, making it clear that she did not approve of being left on the docks with no instructions of how to proceed or expectation of his return.

He gave her a cold nod and offered his arm. "Shall we? The men have been assembled to give you a proper welcome." She hated how he did that—managing to offer seemingly benign information with a scold for her. He'd not been abandoning her; he'd been preparing the way for her. It was a reminder, too, that she needed to trust him even though he was a stranger to her.

The girls fell in behind them as they made their way up the gangplank. "The men are anxious to meet the major's wife," he offered quietly at her ear, another reminder that she wasn't just Mrs. Sheffield now, but the wife of an officer and that people would look to her to set an example. Moira hoped she was up to it. She'd spent so many years setting a bad example. But these men didn't know her. They didn't run in her circles. She stepped on board with the realization that the blank slate the major had talked about the day he'd proposed started now, the moment she set foot on the *Loo Choo*.

There was an instant, snapping rustle as the men came to attention, forming a gauntlet of saluting soldiers for her and the girls to pass through. Moira's first reaction was that there were so many men! There were men lined behind the gauntlet, filling the deck of the big ship as far as she could see. "Where are the women?" she whispered to the major.

"Perhaps belowdecks settling in," he whispered back. "There are a few wives who are acting as laundresses, but nothing more. The other officers' wives are on the other two ships." He halted and raised his voice. "Company H, I present to you my wife, Mrs. Moira Sheffield, and my daughters, Miss Margaret and Miss Lizzie Sheffield. They are in our care for the duration of the voyage. I expect them to be dazzled with the gentlemanly manners of Company H."

One man stepped forward, his posture ramrod

straight, his salute never wavering as he answered for the group. "Yes, sir! On behalf of Company H, ma'am, welcome aboard."

This was followed by a raising of voices in a chorus of unified huzzahs. When the chorus had finished, the major escorted her down the gauntlet, introducing each of his officers. "This is Major Cort Visser." He introduced the man who'd come forward. "This is Captain John Frisbie, First Lieutenant Edward Gilbert, Second Lieutenants John Day and Thomas Elliott, Sergeants Eleazer Frisbie, William Grow, Henry Schoolcraft and James Winne, and Private George Cornwell."

Moira made small talk with each of the ten men, making them smile. Second Lieutenant Elliott even managed a smart rejoinder and gave her a commiserating wink behind the major's back. By the time introductions were done, Moira's head was swimming with names and ranks. How would she ever keep them straight?

If Gemma was here, she'd tell her it was no different from memorizing a guest list or a table seating, the issue of precedence similar to ranking dinner guests. Perhaps she'd make a list once she was settled, imagining the officers around her brother's dinner table. In truth, she couldn't really imagine these men around such a table in such circumstances. They were young, none of them considerably older than she was, and quite a few of them were younger. The major had intimated as much when he'd described the men, but somehow that youth hadn't factored into the visual image she'd made of them in her mind. Neither had their inexperience.

When she'd looked beyond the officers into the ranks behind them, she'd seen just how green these "men" were. They were not soldiers; they were volunteers who were trying to be soldiers. It made her wonder what had happened in their young lives to make them want to leave New York and go to California. Were they, like her, looking for a blank slate? A place where they could forget their pasts and have opportunities New York couldn't give them? She wasn't so naive or sheltered she didn't know what those reasons might be: trouble with the law, poverty and the hopelessness that goes with it.

The major escorted them belowdecks to the cabins. It was hot there. Moira felt the change in temperature immediately. The air was hot *and* still, already carrying a fetid quality to it. Out of the corner of her eye she saw Maggie raise a handkerchief to her nose out of practicality and, no doubt, protest.

If the major noticed his daughter's actions, he was choosing to ignore them just as the Reverend MacVickar had chosen to ignore Maggie's outburst earlier. That's how men coped with women they didn't know how to handle. They ignored them. Hadn't that been what had happened with her? When her brother simply hadn't known what to do with her, he'd ignored her right up until the point he couldn't. And where had that led? To a crisis, then to a sudden marriage. Someone needed to deal with Maggie immediately and it was quite apparent that someone was going to have to be her.

The major held open a door and allowed the three of them to pass inside. "This is your cabin," he said to the girls. To Moira he said, "I thought it would be best if you stayed with them."

"You've decided?" Moira murmured quietly. Her recently settled hackles pricked again. She didn't disagree with the decision, only the process with which it had been made. She'd not been consulted. This had been determined for her. What else had been decided for her?

"Yes, I am not comfortable with the thought of leaving them alone at night," he answered in equally polite, equally quiet tones that addressed her challenge quite sternly. "It's the larger of the two cabins. There's a porthole that will open for fresh air. My cabin is just across the corridor." The cabin his wife wouldn't be sharing with him. But the girls' presence offered a convenient explanation for that should any of the crew notice and think it odd.

"*She's* staying with us? In this cramped space? There's barely room for Lizzie and me," Maggie pouted. The space was indeed small. There was a set of bunks against one wall and a single bed against the other, leaving a bolted-down trunk in the center between them. There was no straight-through access to the porthole. One had to weave between the trunk and the beds to reach it.

Lizzie was already climbing the ladder to the top bunk. "I want this bed!"

"You can have it. I don't want any of these beds and I don't want her in here with us!" Maggie was working up a full head of steam. Moira slid her gaze toward the major. Did he see that an explosion was imminent?

"Margaret Louise, I will not have insubordination from you. Wipe that look off your face. It's all been settled." Displeasure emanated from the major. "You will apologize to me and to your stepmother for those remarks."

"She is not our mother of any sort." Maggie had clearly inherited not only her father's looks but his stern tenacity as well. It made for a poor combination in a battle of father-daughter wills. Did Maggie realize her father could not back down as much for her sake as for his? That she was pushing him into a position he didn't want to be in but would take for his pride as a parent? It would be an ominous note on which to start the voyage. She knew how these things went. The major would regret it the moment he exerted his prerogative and Maggie would be mortified. Mortification could be a damaging thing in a young adolescent girl.

It wasn't just for Maggie and the major that she stepped forward. It was for herself, too. She did not want to set a precedent where the major was her only defense with the girls. She wanted the major's support in raising the girls, but not his protection. It would be a poor family indeed if the major had to act as go-between and mediator for his wife and children. It was time to begin as she meant to go on.

Moira stepped forward as best she could in the cramped space, putting herself between Maggie and the major. She infused her voice with steel so that the major didn't argue with her or that Maggie misunderstood her intentions. She wasn't looking to protect Maggie, or to soften the major's order on her behalf, thinking to win. "Major, if you would excuse us, I'll speak with Maggie and see that the girls are settled."

The major shot her a speaking glance, a golden brow arched in speculation.

"I am sure the men have need of you, Major. You needn't worry about us. I have things well in hand." He nodded at her assurances and left. At least she hoped she had things in hand. This was her Rubicon and she was going to cross it.

Chapter Eight

"Girls, I think it's time the three of us had a little talk." Moira faced Maggie and Lizzie, hands on hips. Suddenly, facing the gauntlet of officers and memorizing their names and rank seemed a far less daunting task than facing two young girls.

Lizzie climbed down and sat on the lower bunk, properly subdued by her tone. She would claim that as progress. But Maggie glared at her from the porthole end of the cabin, arms crossed in defiance. She looked like her father when she tipped her chin up like that. "We don't have to listen to her, Lizzie." Maggie spoke to her sister without her gaze ever leaving Moira's. "She's not—"

"Your mother. I know, you've mentioned it at least twice today," Moira cut in swiftly, answering Maggie's challenge. "Fortunately, this is something we agree on. I am not your mother. I am not looking to replace her." Her words surprised Maggie enough to silence her for the moment. Maggie had expected conflict, not agreement, not common ground. "Nor do I want to take her place. No one can. It would be an impossible task." Moira managed a smile for both of the girls. "However, I would like to be your friend. It's going to be a long voyage. I think all three of us could use a friend or two."

"I think a friend sounds nice," Lizzie offered timidly, looking from Moira to her sister. "I miss my friends already and we've only been gone a few days."

Moira took the tiny olive branch in Lizzie's comments. "We can write your friends letters from our ports of call and when we're settled in California, they can write back."

The younger girl brightened at the idea but Maggie shook her head. "It's a trap, Lizzie. Don't listen to her. What she really wants is to be in charge, to make sure we obey her. She'll make rules we'll have to follow." She shot Moira a nasty look. "That's not what real friends do."

Moira remained calm. "Rules are only necessary when people lack the discipline to control themselves." How many times had her brother used that line with her when he'd had to address another of the scrapes she'd gotten into? The problem with rules was that they had to be enforced. If she made rules, she had to stick to them. Her brother had not been very good at that part. She'd always found a way around him until, at some point, he'd stopped trying to enforce them at all. She'd won but it had turned out to be a hollow victory.

"Are you suggesting I lack self-control?" Maggie looked affronted, the image of grand haughtiness. "Grandmother says I'm a veritable model of femininity." That sounded like something Grandmother Sheffield would say. Moira could hear the old woman's words in her head.

"Yes, I am suggesting just that," Moira agreed, catching Maggie by surprise again. Maggie wanted conflict, wanted to oppose something, and Moira wasn't giving her a chance to carve out any ground. Moira forged ahead. "A proper young lady doesn't speak to her father as you did just now." Nor did a proper young lady conduct herself as Maggie had that morning or on the shopping trip. Moira knew this all too well from experience, and while her heart went out to the girl sympathetically, Moira also knew in hindsight just what such behavior could lead to if left unchecked.

"You don't know anything about me," Maggie shot back.

Oh, but she did. Moira felt she knew this poor girl right down to her toes. She'd felt as Maggie had, acted as Maggie had when she'd been that age. There'd been no one to guide her, no one to truly take her in hand when she'd needed it the most. Grandmother Sheffield had spoiled the girls shamelessly, and who knew how involved their father had been in their upbringing these past three years, which rather surprised Moira.

"Maggie, you shouldn't say such things," Lizzie whispered, wide-eyed, appalled by her sister's behavior. "Father says we should be nice to, to…" Lizzie scrunched up her face and turned it toward Moira. "What should we call you if we don't call you Mama?" It clearly bothered the little girl that she hadn't a name for this new person in her life.

"Why not just call me by my name? Moira." It was the best she could come up with. Both of her parents had died. She'd not been faced with the possibility that her father would remarry and present another mother figure to their household. But she could imagine how she would have felt about it. While she wasn't sure what the girls should call her, she was sure about how they would not want to refer to her: Mother, Step-mama or Mama Moira. All those names would sound too much like a replacement for the mother they'd loved and lost.

Lizzie seemed to think it over and come to a conclusion. "Moira. Just Moira." She nodded, satisfied. "I like that." Maggie rolled her eyes but there was little to argue with.

"Does that work for you, Maggie?" Moira wouldn't make the mistake the reverend and the major made and ignore her, although it would be easier to focus on the progress with Lizzie. But that would only make Maggie more difficult to work with and to reach later.

"What works for me is for you to stop pretending you know me, that you have any clue as to how I feel. You *don't* know me, you're not like me."

"But I am like you. Maybe not *just* like you, but I have some experience with what you're going through," Moira argued patiently. "I lost both of my parents when I was ten. I was angry about it for a long time. I think I still am," Moira admitted, giving Maggie honesty. Perhaps Maggie would respect that in place of sugarcoating.

Moira sat beside Lizzie on the narrow bunk, leaving a space on her other side for Maggie if she chose to join them. "In my anger I made choices that I might have made differently if I'd had a friend to guide me." She could see that in hindsight. Brandon had tried his best but he'd been twenty and awash in his own troubles coping with handling the business, the money, the debt, the properties their father had left behind and the funeral all at once. At the critical moments, there'd been little time to spend on a sister ten years his junior.

"How did they die?" Lizzie asked. Even Maggie looked slightly curious.

"A carriage accident," Moira began. There, in the stuffy little cabin, she unfolded the tragedy that had defined her childhood. It was a story, she realized, she'd not told anyone. No one had ever asked her. Plenty of people had asked Brandon, especially in the early days when society was curious about the sudden deaths of the shipping magnate and his wife. But no one had ever asked her. No one asked ten-year-olds. Perhaps she needed to tell the story as much as the girls needed to hear it.

"My parents were away. They were upstate to

commemorate the opening of a hospital. My father was on the board of directors. But the ceremony had run late and they were traveling in the dark in order to make up time. Their coach hit something in the road—a rock, a rut—whatever it was, the coach hit it just right and they flipped over. The driver survived but my parents were killed instantly. Their necks snapped." Even now it was hard to say the words. Lizzie gasped beside her. Perhaps she'd been too graphic for an eight-year-old.

"My mama died from a fever," Lizzie offered and Moira was surprised to feel a little hand slip inside hers. "We didn't get to see her. Grandmother was afraid we might catch it, too."

"Fevers can be tricky that way," Moira said softly. "I'm sure your grandmother did the right thing." Just because Grandmother Sheffield disapproved of her didn't mean she'd disparage the woman to her granddaughters. She might be wild and reckless by New York society standards, but she wasn't malicious.

"I wish I could have seen her one more time." Lizzie leaned her head against Moira's arm and Moira took the weight with a sense of gratitude she hadn't felt for a long while. Had God finally listened to a prayer? Albeit a small one. *If so, Lord, thank You for this.*

Moira looked over at Maggie. This part was just for her. She hoped the girl would appreciate it, that it wouldn't be a case of throwing pearls before swine. These were her dearest stories, locked away for years. "I was mad at the whole world, even mad at God. How dare a good God let something so senseless as a rut in the road take my parents? They were good people. They helped others, they went to church. They were supposed to be there for me. Now, no one was there for me. My brother didn't have the time for me that I needed. So, I did things to get his attention, to make him make time for me."

"Like what?" Maggie asked cautiously. Did Moira imagine it or had she moved a little closer from the window?

"I stole a boy's clothes from the swimming hole near our summer estate." Moira winced. It had seemed a grand prank eleven years ago. "He had to walk home naked and explain what had happened." She shook her head. "I'm embarrassed about it now. How hard that must have been for him. I did it because I was mad he wouldn't let me come fishing with him and the other boys, but he didn't deserve it."

There were too many things in her adolescence that she didn't like to look back on too often or scrutinize too closely for fear of what she'd find—the actions of a lonely, perhaps selfish girl. Would Maggie see herself in that story? Acting out because things didn't go her way? Because she couldn't reconcile herself to the decisions being made around her? Because she needed to claim attention and through that attention assurance that all would be well?

"I was alone, girls. You don't have to be." This was what she wanted, needed, the girls to know today in order for them all to make a beginning together. She didn't fool herself that a relationship would be built in a day any more than Rome was. Trust took time. Respect took time. Relationships took time. Time was the one they had. They had seventeen thousand miles to travel and six months on board a ship.

From her post, Maggie seemed to relax. "Do I have to say I'm sorry?"

"*Are* you sorry?" Moira asked.

"Not yet," Maggie said but there was no anger behind it, just honesty. "I am still mad at my father for upending us, for making us go to California with him, and for marrying without even asking us." There it was again, that anger over being ignored. She'd not been consulted. Instead, she'd been overridden. Something close to tears shimmered in Maggie's eyes. She was trying valiantly not to let them spill.

"You can apologize when you're ready," Moira said. "It won't mean anything otherwise."

"I might not ever be ready." Maggie's defiance flared momentarily, perhaps in an attempt to quell the threatening tears.

"It's alright if you don't know today." Moira was content to reserve that battle for another time. Right now, the girls and she needed a change of activity. "We have trunks to unpack. I have some curtains in my trunk. What do you think about hanging them up at the porthole to make this place look a little more homey?"

She kept the girls busy. They spent the remainder of the day unpacking trunks, learning to be creative with their space in the cabin and touring the ship. They ate a dinner of roast chicken with fresh potatoes and peas, with a slice of apple pie for each of them brought to their cabin and served on a white cloth by the cook himself at the major's request.

It was thoughtful of the major to take time to think of them while his mind was occupied with more immediate duties. Moira had planned on having to hunt out the galley and bring dinner back herself. After a quick grace to bless the food, Moira had instructed the girls to enjoy it. It would be a long time before food was as fresh as this again.

As night fell, they took a final tour of the deck and a last view of the city beyond before she put the girls to bed. All of this had been accomplished without a reappearance from the major. While she'd been touched by the supper he sent, she'd been disappointed not to see the major himself at dinner, for the girls' sake. With Maggie and Lizzie settled, Moira went to seek out her errant husband. She started with a knock on his cabin door.

"The major isn't there," a friendly drawl informed her from the narrow corridor.

Moira turned toward the voice. "Second Lieutenant Thomas Elliott, isn't it?" She recognized him from earlier in the day. That little ceremony seemed as long ago as her wedding.

"Very good, you've an excellent memory for names." He swept her a bow, his green eyes twinkling. "Or perhaps I might flatter myself that I made an impression?"

Moira laughed. "You may do as you like, Lieutenant. Do you know where my husband is?"

"Tut, tut, married only a day and the bubble is already off the wine? You've lost track of him rather quickly," Lieutenant Elliott teased, but there was a sharp edge that undercut his banter. She'd flirted with enough men to recognize flirting from insidious insinuation and she did not like what the lieutenant might be implying.

"It's a big ship and my husband is a busy man," Moira replied with a loyalty to the major that surprised her. This was how it would be, though. Whether she liked it or not, in public she must always have her husband's back the way he'd had hers in the tearoom against Mrs. Bostwick.

Lieutenant Elliott flashed her a handsome smile. "Forgive me, Mrs. Sheffield, I did not mean to offend." His smile was so winsome she felt she might have overreacted. "Your husband is up on deck. Shall I take you up?" He offered her his arm as if they were about to stroll through a park on Sunday.

"No, thank you," Moira declined. "I am sure I can find him myself." She also wanted a moment to herself, a chance to be alone with her thoughts after a day of being surrounded by people and in close quarters.

She was just starting to understand what it meant to be a mother to these girls. The first of those lessons was that they were with her always. For someone who'd been left to her own devices, engaging in society when she wished and organizing her time as she saw fit, it was a rather rude awakening. Private time, it seemed, had become a thing of the past. Moira had no doubt it would be the first of many changes.

Chapter Nine

Moira found the major at the rail, staring toward the dark bulk of the battery where the city met the harbor. He was still dressed in his uniform as he had been all day. Had he been working all this time? What a long day he must have had, first with getting her and the girls to the ship and then with preparing his men to sail tomorrow. And yet, he'd taken time to make sure they'd boarded the ship with all the respect due them.

"Have you eaten?" she asked, coming up behind him. If not, she wasn't sure what she might do about it. If they'd been at home on Elm Street, she would have ordered cook to fix him a tray. She wasn't sure she had the authority to do that here, though.

"What?" He turned, startled from his thoughts. "Eaten? Oh yes, I ate with the other officers. It's common practice."

"I'm glad you've eaten. I thought you might join

us for dinner. I think the girls missed you." She didn't want to rebuke him but she did want him to know his presence would have been appreciated. If she had to share him with his men, his men had to share him with his family.

He shook his head, dismissing her concern. "I doubt the girls missed me. They're used to dining without me. At West Point, I ate in the mess. Instructors and cadets all ate together. Except for the weekends, of course, when I would visit."

Moira took up a position beside him and leaned on the rail. "This isn't West Point. The girls are out of their depth. Everything is new and unfamiliar to them, even me."

"And yet familiarity breeds contempt. Does Maggie still despise me?" The major slanted her a look.

"You are a convenient target for an adolescent girl's disappointment in the world in general," Moira offered. "You've stripped away all that she knows. It's a lot of change to process all at once. She is sailing into the unknown."

"We all are." The major didn't find that sufficient evidence for rebellion.

"These men are volunteers. They chose this. She didn't. She'll need time to come around but what she doesn't need is to be ignored. Do not leave her to her own devices or she will continue to rebel. She needs your attention and your assurances. They both do."

The major turned to study her, his blue eyes serious. "Is that spoken from a position of authority on the subject?" Something akin to mischief sparked in his serious depths.

Moira felt some of the tension in her ease. "Yes, quite so, Major. I'm more of a firsthand authority on the subject than I'd like to be."

A quick smile quirked at his lips. "You're a lucky person, though, to understand oneself well enough to know it. Some people spend all their lives trying to figure themselves out." He paused and his gaze moved back to the black blob of the city. "How did the rest of the day go?"

Moira gave him an account of their efforts to unpack and decorate and their tours of the ship deck. She couldn't help but wonder if this was a pattern for how their evenings would go. She'd find him on deck and offer him a report of his children as if she were another of his officers. It was a rather impersonal image, and one that she found didn't sit well with her, although it should have. The major had promised her a white marriage, a marriage without the imposition of the marital bed. Their marriage was *meant* to be impersonal. She ought not be offended when he stood by his bargain.

"I am glad you and the girls have come to an accord," he said when she finished. There was so much more she wanted to tell him but his demeanor suggested conversation about the girls was done. He didn't want to hear about Maggie's resentment over not being consulted or that Lizzie had been concerned about what to call her. He'd wanted only the facts: that the girls were sleeping, they'd eaten well and been kept busy, that all was ready for weighing anchor in the morning. Was he that unfeeling? Or was he that clueless about raising his own children? Or was his detachment fueled by something deeper? It was a reminder of how little she knew of the man she'd married.

"Moira, what of yourself? Are you ready to sail? Ready for our adventure?" The question was asked so sincerely, it caught her off guard. One moment he'd been the strict, dispassionate major and the next he was inquiring about her welfare.

"As ready as can be expected. Ready or not, it's going to happen. I imagine I'm not the only one on board tonight who feels that way. The 'men' are young."

"I told you they would be. Young and untrained. They knew nothing of military life and discipline when they came to the island in July. It was chaos at best." He slid a small smile.

"Like me?" Moira dared. She, too, knew nothing of military life and discipline. Perhaps she was a kind of chaos to him as well despite his arguments to the contrary.

"And yet, both you and my men comported themselves well today." There was a compliment in that for her. He meant the welcoming ceremony, and a certain flush of pride suffused her. It pleased her that she'd pleased him in some small way, especially when she knew she'd disappointed him in others. He turned to face her. "Moira, might you do something for me? Would you call me by my name? Ben or even Benjamin would suffice. But not Major, not when we're alone."

"Of course," she acceded easily even as internally she counseled herself to patience, which was not her strong suit.

This husband of hers was proving to be a conundrum. Just when she was ready to classify him as a hard man, more interested in his career than in the people around him, he would do something that demonstrated his humanity, that proved there was a strong streak of innate kindness in him, that he was very much a man as opposed to an automaton; the way he'd kissed her at the wedding, the way his hands had felt when he'd helped her with her dress last night, the way he'd inquired about her readiness just now, the way he hungered to hear someone say his name. All of which suggested that there was indeed a man beneath the uniform, beneath the fortress he'd erected around himself. She wanted to know that man. He seemed a far more interesting fellow than the stern major. Perhaps that man could be set free if he could just be reached.

Please, Lord, let me reach him, let me find that man. That made two prayers in two days. It was quite a lot for a girl who'd not prayed in years, not seriously anyway. What had been the point? God didn't listen. God had taken her parents for no reason. Perhaps it was a sign of how desperate she was, willing to cast about for any support. It invoked other thoughts, too. Why did she care if she reached the man within? What did that matter to her?

"Moira, what are you doing?" came his quiet question.

"Nothing. Wishing on a star," she lied. Once upon a time she would have expected a bolt of lightning to strike her for such a lie. That was before she'd decided God, like everyone else, had little time for her. He didn't have time to notice the perfidies of a ten-year-old, just as he hadn't had time to save that ten-year-old's parents. She was still mad about that. Like Maggie, she wasn't quite ready to apologize yet.

Silence stretched between them. They'd discussed the girls and the day. What else was there to talk about? "Shall I escort you below? We sail at sunrise, another early day for us all," the major—no, *Ben*—asked.

"I can see myself down." She smiled and then added with a soft touch on his sleeve, "Don't stay up too late, *Ben*. You need your sleep, too."

That touch stayed with him long after Moira had gone below. He lingered on deck already knowing he would have trouble sleeping tonight despite the long day. Ben could feel it in his bones. The old, anxious excitement thrummed through him. It had felt this way the night before he'd marched out to Fort Brady, the night before his wedding to Sarah, the night Sarah had told him she was expecting their first child. Those had been eves of change.

This was another eve of change. Tomorrow, he set out for a new land, a new life. The excitement wouldn't last, he knew that, too, from experience.

The march to Fort Brady had been wet and muddy and full of obstacles. The excitement had soon paled, as would the excitement of this voyage. His men were barely ready for the expedition. There would be disobedience to deal with as a result. When the journey grew long and the ennui of the sea set in, there'd be pranks and other forms of minor rebellion. There would be his new wife to contend with as well.

She'd been a revelation today in her black-and-white-striped gown and matching hat with ribbons that floated on the air. The gown had suited her and the occasion. No man seeing her would mistake her for anything other than a lady. That was exactly the tone he wanted to strike with the formality of his family's entrance. There were few women aboard and long voyages had a certain effect on men deprived of female company. He didn't want anyone directing those frustrations toward his wife. His men needed to respect his wife; they didn't need to like her. In fact, he preferred they didn't like her, not in that way.

He'd prefer he not like her in *that* way either but that was becoming a difficult battle. She was stunning with all that dark hair and those flashing eyes. She had enough height to command the attention of a room and an elegant, slim build that would keep that attention once gained. It was no wonder every swain in New York society aspired to her in some manner, and no wonder that they'd been rebuffed. Moira Blackthorne—*Sheffield*, he reminded himself—was a law unto herself.

Although she'd trembled last night when he'd touched her, a reminder that for all her bravado, her understanding of the world of men was still limited to ballrooms and stolen kisses. There was a virtuous woman beneath the hellion's exterior. He was attracted to both. The hellion had masterfully dismissed him this afternoon, preferring to take his recalcitrant daughter in hand herself, much as she'd taken the arrogant Edward Brant in hand. That had impressed him. It had been exactly what he'd hoped for. Maggie needed more than he was capable of giving her, so he'd given her Moira instead.

There was going to be a price for that, though. He hadn't just wanted Moira for the girls. That wild part of him that wanted the adventure of California wanted her for himself while that decent, upstanding other part of him felt guilty for the wanting of her, the wanting of a new start. It chastised him daily and nightly; how dare he take his girls from the civilized home of his mother, the bucolic surroundings of West Point, the luxuries that could be provided by his mother's family's connections. How dare he trade all that for California simply because he was hungry for adventure? Because he thought he deserved adventure? Deserved to resurrect old hungers and dreams? He'd promised Sarah to keep them safe. How dare he marry society's most unsuitable girl when he'd once had the perfect wife? The perfect love? What did that say about the sacredness of Sarah's memory that he would seek to find a wife who was reckless, who questioned his authority?

The answer came too readily, and too embarrassingly simply: because once he'd seen Moira, he'd not been able to look away. Today alone, she'd irritated him at the docks, then moments later pleased him upon greeting his officers, upon taking his daughters in hand. Then irritated him with her cool challenges about his absence at dinner, before laying her hand on his sleeve and sending a river of awareness up his arm—an awareness he was not ready to acknowledge until his conscience was clear. Nor could he act upon it without violating his promise, not unless she, too, changed her mind about the conditions of their marriage.

Ben laughed out loud in the darkness. He'd been a married man for one day and already he was being tempted to forgo his promises. He would have to steel his resolve if he was going to survive six months at sea with this particular siren. Perhaps it was what he deserved when he chose to wed a woman in haste.

Chapter Ten

The sail away could have gone better, Ben mused from his position at the rail as the *Loo Choo* slipped in the narrows and rounded Sandy Hook, leaving Governor's t Island and New York City behind *well after* sunrise. Perhaps the botched departure was no less than the pompous Colonel Stevenson deserved for having overinflated the import of the mission. Despite the early hour, Stevenson had seen to it that the three transport ships sailed out with a bang from a two-cannon salute from Fort Columbia and a musical sendoff from a bleary-eyed band on the docks playing "The Girl I Left Behind."

Not that there was anyone to hear it. Which was probably for the best given that when the steamers arrived to tow the ships out of the harbor, the current was against them and they had to wait for the ebb tide. Perhaps Stevenson shouldn't have acceded to the men's request to not sail on Friday. The colonel clearly had not checked the tide charts to determine the impact of the delay. It was a dismal start to the venture after the hoopla of the sendoff. Ben could only imagine what the *Tribune* would make of it in the editorials that ran today, reminding the public that no matter how loudly Stevenson and the *Herald* proclaimed the patriotic magnificence of the mission, this was nothing more than trumped-up manifest destiny.

What would Moira say? She'd say, "Let the *Tribune* do its worst. We won't see their editorials." Moira didn't give a whit for what people thought and today he wouldn't either. He'd be miles away, out on the open sea before the *Tribune*'s scathing remarks hit the newsstands. There was some joy in that thought. No matter the debacle of the departure or the politics surrounding the regiment's founding or the dubious quality of men actually recruited for what was supposed to have been an elite assemblage of New York's finest manhood, for him, the adventure was beginning at last.

He was more honest with himself than Stevenson was. These men wouldn't see action in the war with Mexico. They were settlers in uniform, an army of occupation only. He thanked God for that. He wouldn't have considered taking his daughters into a war zone. His men certainly weren't up for war, either. But he had hope for these young men. Of all the regiments, the *Loo Choo* companies were made up of the more educated and literarily minded recruits. In his more optimistic moments, Ben liked to think these men would be the new territory's journalists, writers and mayors.

At the sound of the bugle, Ben turned from the rail and set aside his fantasizing. The journey had just begun. They were a long way from California and even further from the day they would all be mustered out and set free to pursue their dreams. He straightened his shoulders and tugged down his jacket. It was time to inspect the troops and get on with the day's work. Today was the first of 164 days between New York and California, give or take for ports of call and weather. Best to begin as he meant to go on. The sooner a routine was established, the better for all of them.

That routine came soon enough. The days fell into an ordered pattern of drills, chores and reports. The convoy picked up the southwest trades and sailed into the Mid-Atlantic with haste. Water stretched in all directions for days on end. His men held up well under the rigors and the eternal sameness of life at sea. Ben took pride in that accomplishment, especially when news came from the other two ships via men rowing over in dinghies for the daily exchange of reports. His fellow West Pointer, Lieutenant Colonel Burton, on the *Susan Drew* had to put down a minor mutiny over the required regulations regarding bathing, which resulted in hats and the guardhouse being thrown overboard. Colonel Stevenson had a rather larger mutiny threaten over the punishment meted out to a sergeant who disobeyed orders from his superiors. There was nothing that serious aboard the *Loo Choo*.

His men weren't the only ones settling in. His daughters had done admirably. Maggie had not complained since leaving New York and Moira dedicated a large part of the day to lessons up on deck when the weather was fair. It did his heart good to be able to look over at the space Moira had claimed as an outdoor classroom and see his girls, heads bent over slates or books, Moira's dark head bent with them.

At a distance, all seemed bucolic. That was how he saw the girls—at a distance. He was involved in the business of running troops on a ship, working through reports from the quartermaster regarding supplies, and reports from his officers about the men's health, behaviors and needs. He took his meals with the other officers in order to build relationships with them and their men through them.

In the evenings, Moira reported to him on the girls' progress. He looked forward to those reports, not just hearing about his daughters but in seeing the woman who delivered those messages. Being at sea agreed with her. She was busy each day and, to his relief, whatever wildness she'd demonstrated in New York had not made an appearance since they'd sailed. Their conversations in the evening were congenial. They would talk over the lessons and how the girls were doing. She would share stories from the day that would make him laugh, like how Lizzie had tried to balance her pencil between her nose and her lip, or how Second Lieutenant Thomas Elliott had stopped to help the girls with a lesson in French.

"I can help with French," Ben had volunteered automatically and perhaps defensively. Elliott was a flatterer. To which Moira had answered quite pointedly, "Yes, you could, the girls would love to see you." That was one area of contention between them. In her oft-voiced opinion, he needed to make more time for Maggie and Lizzie. To which he answered it was important that she and the girls establish a close bond. If he was in the way, that might deter the girls from looking to her for guidance. After all, once they were in California, he might be away from home quite a bit on army business.

In truth, being with his daughters brought his old life, his old grief, too close. Sarah would be so proud of the girls. How many nights did he wish she could see them? Lizzie was her very image, and Maggie was becoming a beautiful young woman with a caring soul, just as lovely inside as she was outside. Maggie, who had taken it upon herself to care for Lizzie so generously in the early days after Sarah's death, Maggie, whose fierce temper had not yet forgiven him for leaving New York. Although, Moira seemed to have that temper in check. He loved his daughters but it was best to love them at a distance for fear of letting his grief swamp him.

The other piece they argued about was Second Lieutenant Elliott. Too often, Moira's tales of the day included some reference to him. The lieutenant, it seemed, made a regular appearance at lessons, offering tutelage in a variety of subjects. Moira had remarked several times how helpful it was since it allowed her to work with one of the girls in a more focused manner without feeling as if she was neglecting the other one. At first, he'd wondered if that was Moira's way of pointing out she'd prefer that he be the one dropping by lessons to help. Now, he fought the urge to cringe every time the lieutenant's name was mentioned.

Was he really jealous because the man spent more time with his girls and his wife than he did? He could spend all the time he wanted with them if he chose to, he reminded himself. He found himself contemplating whether he should reassign the lieutenant to a different shift so that he wouldn't be near Moira when the girls did their lessons. No, he would not be so petty. Such a passive-aggressive maneuver smacked of David's actions against Uriah, all to clear the path to the delectable Bathsheba. He would not stoop so low. Would Moira? Did she want him to be jealous? Did she bring up the man's name so often because she wanted to point out that she held the man's attention? Surely not. She had no interest in making him jealous. Their marriage wasn't like that, which made his own jealousy as absurd as the idea of her seeking to cultivate it.

"You look deep in thought." Cort Visser joined him at the quarterdeck, where they had a clear view of Moira and the girls doing lessons in the autumn sun. They were just a few days out of Rio de Janeiro and the warmer weather of the equator, the first place they'd put in for water and some much-needed shore leave. "How's married life?" Cort's gaze followed his own trajectory to Moira and the girls.

"Fine, why do you ask?"

Cort shrugged. "You don't spend the kind of time with your new bride that a bridegroom would. The men have noticed."

Ben felt his jaw tighten. "I have obligations and the girls can't be left alone. An army transport ship isn't the most ideal place for a honeymoon." He cleared his throat, uncomfortable at having to justify his behavior. His marriage was his business, not his men's.

"Fort Brady wasn't exactly easy living, either." Cort chuckled and then sobered. "You forget I know you and I knew Sarah. The man you've become is not the man you were."

"It's hardly polite to expose a wife to so much indelicate company. The men all need to keep that in mind It wouldn't hurt them to practice some manners." Ben didn't want to talk about Sarah or Moira, not even with Cort.

Cort gave a little nod. "I'll be sure to mention it the next time it comes up." "I'm sure there's no malice intended." Cort was quick to reframe his comment. "They all love her. They might have been superstitious about sailing on a Friday but they seem to have forgotten any superstitions about having women on board. She makes them want to be better men, all for the hope of her smile, a kind word, a laugh." Cort made a gesture with his hand toward Moira and the girls. "They remind the men of home and family, of the good things in life, pretty things." Ben knew. She reminded him of those things, too, and more. That was what worried him. Cort was being polite. There were other things Moira reminded a man of besides hearth and home.

A blond head joined Moira at the makeshift school space and Ben stiffened. *Elliott.* The man was full of life, always ready with a quick smile and a laugh. He was a lot like Moira that way and the very opposite of Ben himself. Would Moira prefer a laughing husband? For a moment envy pierced Ben. He pushed it away. Jealousy was poorly done of him. He could choose to smile more if he wanted to and he should not begrudge Moira a friendship. And yet, deep down he knew he did, only because he wanted that friendship himself and he knew he had yet to claim it. The fault here was all his, not hers. She was a decent woman no matter her wild streak.

Cort nodded." He looked as if he might say something more and then thought better of it.

Private Winne coughed from a discreet distance to announce his presence. "Major Visser, Major Sheffield, excuse me. Major Sheffield, I have the report from the quartermaster."

"Very good." Ben turned to Cort. "Keep an eye on things for me while I go below."

The lesson was going poorly. Moira was trying to teach the girls a math lesson but was having no success. "What's amiss?" Lieutenant Elliott's long shadow crossed the glare of the sun, his smile easy.

"We're trying to do probabilities, but it isn't making sense," Maggie put in, as exasperated as Moira.

Thomas reached for a slate. "Let's try it this way. Probability is nothing more than the odds of something happening." Moira felt her frustration ease. How nice to have help and competent help at that. Despite his easy outer demeanor that bordered on the flirtatious, Thomas Elliott was well-educated and she welcomed his assistance with lessons. She'd also come to welcome his company. He was always ready with a story for her and the girls, and company on the high seas was in short supply, especially when her husband seemed inclined to provide so little of it. Still, she was always careful to be with him only in the presence of the girls. Beyond that brief encounter in the hall the first night, she was never alone with him or any of the men.

Thomas turned the slate around for the girls to see. He'd drawn a dicing cube. "On any dicing cube, there's a one-sixth chance, or probability, that you'll roll any given number." He pulled a cube from his pocket and passed it to Lizzie. "Roll it." The cube came up with a one. "Alright, now, Miss Maggie, you roll. Does the probability of rolling a one change since we've already rolled that number?"

"No." Maggie shook her head. "There are still six sides, so there are still six chances of it being a one."

Thomas produced a second dice. "Now what are the chances of rolling a one?"

"Two chances out of twelve?" Maggie ventured, earning a praising smile from Thomas.

"So, from this we can conclude that in order to determine probability, we need to divide the frequency of the event by the sample space. In this case, the frequency is the amount of available number ones and the event space is twelve sides of the dice." He winked at Moira. "Shall we see how this works in action? How about an outing to the other end of the ship?"

She probably shouldn't allow it but the girls looked so excited and after an afternoon of failed lessons, Moira was eager to hang on to this piece of success. Besides, entertainment and change were hard to come by in the middle of the ocean. She could scarcely deny the girls this small treat of breaking their monotony.

"They're playing Liar's Dice," Thomas announced when they reached a group of off-duty men at the other end. The men grinned up at them but seemed uneasy. These were the major's daughters and the major's wife. "We're learning probability today," Thomas explained, putting them at ease. "I thought we might give them some practice."

The men made room for them and someone passed Moira a cup with five dice inside.

"So, now we have to calculate the probability based on five dice. Can you do it?" she asked the girls.

They rolled their cup and studied the dice beneath it. "Remember, each die has a one-sixth chance of being any given number," Moira coached. "Which means there's a five-sixths chance that it won't be. And the dice are independent of each other," Her own mind was starting to whir with possibilities, reveling in the mental exercise of one-sixth multiplied by one-sixth multiplied by five-sixths multiplied by five-sixths multiplied by five-sixths to determine the probability of rolling two of the same number.

She let the girls calculate quietly on their slates and decide when to call for the lie. They did well, only losing one of their dice as the men lost theirs and fell out of the game. It was down to Thomas, Moira and the girls and a man named Sammie from Company H, and the game had become intense, drawing a crowd. Moira and the girls had four of their dice left, Thomas had three and Sammie had one.

"Three fives." Sammie made a bold, reckless bid, suggesting there were three fives among the remaining eight dice.

"We should call him out," Lizzie hissed fiercely beside her. "There's no way almost half of the dice are all fives."

"The girls are going to take you out of the game, Sammie," a man laughed from behind Moira and a chant went up, "take him out, take him out." Moira shook her head and made her own bid. "One six." She'd rather drive Sammie out of the game this way than to risk whatever Thomas had under his cup.

"Two sixes," Thomas bid.

"Three sixes." Sammie was forced to it and this time Moira pounced.

"Liar!" she called out, flush with impending victory and Sammie sheepishly uncovered his remaining cube to reveal a five. Another cheer went up as the game narrowed to just her and Thomas.

"Alright, it's just us now, Moira." Thomas gave her a wide grin as they rattled their cups and the men pressed close. The girls were giddy with excitement and Moira felt quite in her element. . Suddenly she felt the tight knot of men loosen and disperse, space opening up around her.

"What is going on here?"

Moira looked up into the thunderous face of her husband. She rose quickly to her feet, brushing at her skirts. "I was teaching the girls probability. Just a math lesson." She was careful not to drag anyone else into it. This had been her decision, she'd allowed it. She didn't want anyone else to get into trouble over it. But Thomas stepped in.

"I suggested it, sir." Thomas saluted. "Don't be angry with her or the girls. It was just a bit of fun to make the math lesson more applicable." Moira had only thought her husband had looked thunderous before. Now, he truly was. Thomas's attempt to help had only made things worse in a way she didn't quite understand.

"Applicable? To what?" Her husband's voice was cold steel. "What cause do you think these girls will have to need to know how to wager on Liar's Dice?"

"My mistake, sir." Thomas saluted smartly once more.

"You are dismissed, Lieutenant Elliott. Girls, go

to your cabin. Mrs. Sheffield, please accompany me to my quarters." No eight words in the history of the world had ever ruined an afternoon quite so thoroughly. Moira followed her husband below, her own temper soaring. How dare he treat her like a disobedient child and order her off the deck. If he thought he was going to scold her, he had another thing coming. If anyone asked her, he was the one who needed scolding.

Chapter Eleven

Nothing ruined an afternoon like finding your wife playing Liar's Dice with the crew, excepting finding her playing Liar's Dice with Thomas Elliott and *enjoying* it. She stood before him in the tight confines of his cabin, her hair falling down in a wild tumble of dark waves, her cheeks flushed, all proof of just how much she'd enjoyed it and proof of how unrepentant she was.

"What were you thinking?" he asked with all the stern restraint he could muster. Had she been thinking at all?

"That the girls needed a math lesson, as I've said already. We did not play for money," she replied, her stare boring into his as if he'd been the one to act in error.

"Was that all? Did you at any time think about how this would look to the men? To me?"

A mocking smile flitted across her lips. "How

did it look to you? Apparently, it did not look like a math lesson. Please do explain."

That he could not do. His words had been poorly chosen. He could not tell her how it had appeared to him without exposing too much. "It looked as if my wife was gambling with the crew, exposing my daughters to base entertainment, and enjoying the company of other men."

She was still for a long moment. Another woman would have dropped her eyes and begged forgiveness but not Moira. Penitence was not in her posture. "Well, maybe I was—enjoying the company of others, since I get so little company from you. That they are men is hardly my fault since there isn't any other company to choose from. The other women are on the other ships." Her hands were on her hips, her voice low. "If you would prefer I keep other company, perhaps you should provide it. The girls and I cannot live in isolation for one hundred and sixty-four days, although you seem to have it down to a knack."

"What is that supposed to mean?" Ben felt his jaw tighten.

"That we'd like to see more of you. You spend no time with your daughters except for an occasional turn around the deck, and they miss you. One would think it would be impossible to avoid your own family on a ship for weeks on end, but you've turned it into an art form. Eat your meals with us. You needn't eat all of them, but some of them, a few dinners a week. Surely, the officers' mess will survive without you. Stop by for lessons. You speak three languages, share that with them. You said yourself this was to be a new start but you're just repeating old patterns, starting with foisting Maggie and Lizzie off on me just as you did with your mother. They're delightful girls. They're growing up and you are *absolutely* missing it!"

Moira's voice rose until he was sure anyone in the corridor outside would be able to hear. The last thing he wanted was the men to have any more gossip to spread about the state of his marriage. No, that was the second-to-last thing he wanted. The *last* thing he wanted was to have someone tell him what a poor father he was being. Her words stung with truth but did no one understand what he was up against? He chose to ignore the comment and took refuge in the other issue.

"There's the men to consider. How might this look to them, Moira? The major's wife tossing dice with them, making herself available for their company beyond a few polite words while taking a turn on deck?" He couldn't give her a direct answer so he gave her an indirect one instead, hoping she wouldn't realize it. She didn't realize, at least not yet, because she was too distracted by his latest misstep and was preparing to make him pay for that, too.

"Do you think I am flirting with those men on purpose? Some of them are mere boys, younger than me and only a bit older than Maggie." She was furious now and so was he. How dare she seek to scold him when she'd been the one throwing dice. How dare she tell him how to raise his daughters?

Hot words, words he'd never meant to speak, poured out before he could stop them. "You've got Lieutenant Elliott wrapped around your finger so tight he's willing to take a flogging for you."

"You wouldn't. Lieutenant Elliott has done nothing but stand as my friend." She stared at him in frozen horror for a long moment, until something in her expression melted and a certain, dangerous, female realization dawned in her eyes, quieting the gray storm in them. "Why, Benjamin, you're jealous."

He pushed a hand through his hair in a gesture of denial. "I am a lot of things, Moira. I am mad, I am frustrated. I am watching my plan fall apart. No man likes to admit he's made a mistake. But this is a mistake." He drew a breath. He was not ready to be a husband again. He couldn't even really manage to be a father again yet. His grief was far rawer than he thought. "When we get to Rio de Janeiro, the *Brutus* will meet us there. It's a small, fast ship, and it can take you back to New York."

"A divorce? You want to divorce me?" She sank down on the bunk, in a state of confusion. He'd managed to shock the unshockable Moira and he hated himself for it.

"No, not a divorce. I will give you an annulment," he clarified, thinking that might somehow mitigate the shock.

"And the girls? Will they come with me?" He could see thoughts racing in the flash of her eyes.

"No, they'll stay with me. Perhaps I can find a grandmotherly sort when we put in at Rio who can complete the journey, or one of the officers' wives from one of the other ships." He'd made promises. He could keep that one. But when he looked at Moira, he could see the cost of that promise, made to another woman, to Sarah, the wife of his youth, the mother of his children: to raise the girls in love, to keep them with him, to keep them safe.

But keeping his promise to Sarah was hurting Moira. And that was only part of the hurt. The other part was his words, words that had nothing to do with Sarah or grief or the past and everything to do with himself and his feelings.

Divorce. Annulment. Scandalous words. The whole point of this marriage had been to save her from scandal, not conjure up a new one. Then there was the twin shock of leaving the girls. Moira sank onto the bunk, fury going out of her like the tide as a deeper realization swept her. "*This* is a mistake? You mean *I* am a mistake." She'd hurt him. Just as she'd hurt her brother and in the same ways: often, deeply and unintentionally. This was the pattern of her life. She seemed unable to break it, even with her best intentions.

"No, Moira. *I* made the mistake." There was weariness in his eyes, which she felt responsible for putting there, and what had she done? She'd scolded him.

He must think her a shrew among other things. She hadn't thought how the game would look to him or the men, or how Thomas Elliott's friendship might appear. *She hadn't thought*. That was a common theme with her, it seemed. She hadn't thought how the shooting challenge would look to Edward Brant or to the other party guests.

"I hadn't realized you were so unhappy," Moira began. "I thought things were going well." That was part of her shock, too. Things were going well with the girls. Maggie still had the occasional sulk, but the three of them were getting on and getting to know one another. There was progress there. "I thought I was doing exactly what you wanted. It is something of a surprise to learn that I am not." Perhaps she simply wasn't capable of it, even if she tried. "When were you going to tell me you were disappointed?" For that matter, when was he going to tell her a ship from New York was meeting them in Rio? He discussed nothing with her, not his work, and certainly not his feelings. The reports she delivered each night were one-way exchanges of information. She reported and he listened. "I thought you found my reports satisfactory." More than satisfactory. She'd thought he liked the stories she passed on of the girls' antics.

"I do," he was quick to assure her. "I'm pleased you're all getting along."

"But I am not their governess. I am your wife. Perhaps you wish I was only the former," Moira divined. If she were his employee, she would be easier to manage, easier to dismiss when her services were no longer required.

Something flashed in Ben's blue eyes. "No, I don't wish that at all."

"No, of course not. Governesses don't come with shipping lines."

Ben's temper snapped. "What are you implying?"

"That you weren't quite truthful when you proposed. You said you liked my tenacity. But it's my ships you like. If you send me away, you'll lose my brother's ships for your greengrocery. You needed an heiress, someone who was reckless enough or desperate enough to marry quickly." And there she was, the most reckless and desperate of them all, hanging there like low fruit on the vine ready for plucking.

To his credit, her husband looked stunned. "I did *not* marry you for your brother's ships. Is that what you've been thinking all this time? That I'm a fortune hunter? That I was looking to exploit a woman's connections through marriage? Is that the man you think I am?"

She'd hurt him again with this latest affront to his honor. She knew in that instant her claim wasn't true. She shook her head. That was not the man she thought he was. It was just a convenient frame she'd constructed for herself, something to keep her own hurt at bay when it became clear he was not interested in pursuing a relationship with her. Her hopes had been lifted by that one kiss at the church, the way he'd talked to her at the hotel about the men and the journey and his own career. She'd felt perhaps there could be something in time. But since boarding the ship, it was clear to her in his avoidance that all the intrigue was on her side.

"I'm not sending you away, Moira. I am giving you a chance to go home, to return to your family, to your old life. Isn't that what *you* want?"

"You should ask me what I want instead of deciding it for me," Moira replied firmly, self-awareness flooding her. For the first time, standing there in the tiny cabin, facing her handsome, stoic husband, a man she barely knew, Moira understood what she wanted. She wanted to stay. She wanted to continue getting to know the girls. She wanted to know *him*. "What I want is a chance at the new start you promised me. What I want is a chance to build the friendship you promised me the day you proposed. But I can't do either of those things if you don't let me in, if you treat me like an officer instead of a wife. I want to know you, Ben." *I want to be loved, not commanded.*

The last thought came to her in a sudden, silent onslaught of realization. Was that what she'd been seeking all these years? The right to be loved? Plenty of people had commanded her, ordered her life, right down to whom she would marry. Her mother had loved her. Her father had loved her. Her brother loved her, although in the end he'd been forced to set that love aside for commanding. One did not command love. One cultivated it, grew it slowly over time, her mother had said. One had to give love in order to receive it, even if the return was slow in coming. That was the scary part. What if she reached out, what if Ben didn't return her love?

"You want to stay?" Ben was staring at her as if she'd grown two heads. His tone was soft. The anger had left them both now.

"Yes, I want to stay, but…" She let the word hang between them. "We cannot continue to live separate lives that only intersect for half an hour each evening." Moira drew a deep breath; this next request was a risk. He might deny her. She hoped not. It seemed as if their future would be determined by his response. "Ben, you have to let me in. You can start slowly. I don't need all of your secrets at once but I do need to be included. Tell me about your day, about your work, about our journey, anything at all, just include me." She'd asked for those things for the girls but it was harder to ask those things for herself.

Ben sighed. "We've made a hash of this haven't we?" Yes. They both had, he with his reticence and she with her headstrong stubbornness that had led her to think in the moment without considering the consequences of her actions.

"We have a second chance," Moira offered. "Will you take it?"

Ben gave her a smile. "I will try, Moira. I can't promise perfection. I, my…" He groped for the right words, a surprising occurrence for the confident man she knew. In the end, he settled for, "I've grown used to my own company and counsel, Moira. But I will try."

She gave a soft laugh. "We are alike, Ben. I have

also grown used to my own company and counsel. This is new to me, too. We will help each other." She paused. "Ben, I want to be a good friend to you, if nothing else."

She did. In that moment, she wanted it more than anything. She did not want to disappoint this man, who carried a secret weight within him. She wanted to do more than merely not disappoint. She wanted to be a source of solace and comfort to him as she tried to be for his daughters. The flood of emotion surrounding that thought was new to her. This was no longer about her; it was about them, about putting someone else's needs ahead of her own. New territory indeed for a girl who'd grown up with nothing to consider but herself. It felt frightening and it felt…good.

For a long moment, they stared at one another, awareness prickling between them that an accord had been reached, and with it a new chapter in their relationship had opened. But what to say next? Nothing seemed quite right. She decided to test their new foundations. "Will you join us for dinner?"

Ben smiled. "Absolutely. I would like nothing better." Neither would she, Moira realized. It was a start.

Chapter Twelve

The truce—Ben needed a better word for the situation with Moira; truce implied a temporary peace and this was meant to be something more—had lasted a full week by the time they sailed into Rio. Spirits were high, both his and his men's, as the three ships dropped anchor beside the US warship already in the bay and the fast ship, the *Brutus*, which had caught up with them, carrying the one hundred men who'd accidentally been left behind in New York when the fleet had sailed.

There was much to celebrate, Ben thought as he readied himself in his cabin for the activities of the day. A new baby had been born en route on the *Thomas Perkins* to the wife of one of the officers. The men aboard the *Thomas Perkins* had voted to name the baby girl Alta California out of deference for their mission, and the parents had agreed. Another joy was more practical. The fleet was on schedule, praise the Lord. For all the dire predictions made by the *Tribune*, the little convoy had encountered few of the mishaps that usually beset voyages: no diseases, no outbreaks of scurvy to date, no storms or poor weather, no mechanical crises like the loss of a sail or mast or leaks, knock wood. Of course, there was still a great distance to go. Rio was slightly more than four thousand nautical miles from Manhattan, about 20 percent of their journey. It was only the end of the November and there was still the Cape to round. But, still, Ben found the current success heartening.

He tied his stock with careful precision before putting on his officer's coat. There were blessings to count with Moira as well. Since their row, things between them had been markedly improved, perhaps because his own efforts were improved on that front. He dined *en famille* three nights a week and on Sundays with Moira and the girls. He played checkers or cards with the girls beforehand and strolled Moira about the deck afterward, stargazing with awe at the southern skies.

Those strolls were fast becoming the highlights of his weeks. Neither of them had ever been this far south before and this was new territory for the both of them. They reveled in the novelty of warm weather, amazed that it was summer here in the Southern Hemisphere while it was approaching winter in far-away New York. They were dazzled by the stars, Scorpio and Sagittarius shining bright in the velvet darkness of the night sky. Experiencing these new lands together was a way forward for them, something they could build on and claim as their own memories together.

Today would be another first. Together, they would attend the christening of little Alta California on the *Thomas Perkins*. It would be a public appearance, the two of them together as husband and wife at a social event. He hoped this appearance would put paid to any lingering rumors about the status of his marriage. Ben finished buttoning his coat and took a final brush of his sleeves. It wasn't the public nature of the event alone that had him wanting to look his best. He was aware of a desire to please Moira, that she would take pride in standing beside him. It had been a long time since he'd dressed for a woman's approval.

Satisfied with his appearance, Ben crossed the narrow corridor to Moira's cabin and paused a moment to listen to the chatter within. The sounds of Moira and the girls making ready brought a smile to his face. He knocked and chuckled to himself when there was a sudden, panicked flurry of last-minute preparations on the other side. How feminine it sounded, how domestic and sweet. It brought a man a certain kind of peace to hear his womenfolk chattering, to know they had nothing else to worry about but hair ribbons. He had not thought to feel that kind of peace again.

His. It was a potent word, rife with possession and protection. His daughters had always been his since the moments of their births, but now that designation extended to Moira. She was his by law, of course, although he expected Moira would have some protest to make about that. But each day that went by, she was his in other more meaningful ways than legally. She was the last person he saw at night when he left her at her door and turned in to his own cabin, the person he shared his day with, and the person, who in turn, shared their day with him. There was joy in the receiving of that, of sharing in her stories.

The door opened and Moira stood before him, genteel summer personified in a white gown sprigged with tiny green flowers. She carried a white shawl over one arm and a parasol in her other hand. Her dark waves were done up in a pretty style and threaded with a green ribbon. Another green ribbon held a cameo at her throat. "Will we do?" Moira smiled and stepped out into the corridor, followed by the girls.

Maggie wore a white dress with a blue sash, her blond hair done in long soft curls. Lizzie wore her customary pink but he noted the dress was getting short. Still, Moira had seen to it that the dress was neatly pressed and that Lizzie had a "new" hair ribbon to compensate, courtesy of Moira's own collection, no doubt. Together, the trio stole his breath, his beautiful growing-up girls and Moira, his stunning wife. He offered Moira his arm and his other to his daughters and led them up on deck.

The deck bustled with a festive atmosphere engendered by the change in the daily routine. All the officers would row over in the dinghies to the *Thomas*

Perkins for the baptism while part of the crew would take the remaining dinghies for much-anticipated shore leave. After the baptism, Ben would enjoy a bit of that shore leave with Moira in the market as well. He helped Moira and the girls carefully into the little boat and they were off, covering the short distance between the ships, Lizzie clutching their gift for the new baby tightly to her chest to protect it from the spray.

The baptism went well. Colonel Stevenson had seen to it that there was drink and a small reception afterward so that the officers could mingle among themselves after having not seen each other since leaving New York. Ben took pains to introduce Moira to his fellow West Pointers like Lieutenant Colonel Burton, who was on the *Susan Drew* and hadn't yet had a chance to meet her. Inevitably, though, as often happens at such gatherings, the men and women dispersed to discuss their separate interests. To his pleasure, Moira and the girls did slip from his side to join the other women in admiring the new baby. Female company on the *Loo Choo* was at a minimum. He wanted Moira to meet the other women. She would need their friendship when they all arrived in California. It didn't hurt to start cultivating those relationships as best she could now.

"Your wife is a natural." Cort took up a position at his shoulder, sipping from his tankard. He nodded toward the knot of women gathered around the infant.

Ben opened his mouth to make a comment about

Moira's sociability and then realized that wasn't what Cort meant. Moira stood amid the women, holding Alta California in her arms, Lizzie and Maggie at her sides, a smile on her face unlike any smile she'd offered Ben to date. The baby must have fussed. Moira lifted it and adjusted her position and the baby settled while Moira swayed in place to keep the baby satisfied. Ben felt his heart respond to the sight, filled with a yearning so intense and sudden it bordered on painful. His throat tightened. He remembered feeling that way when the girls were born. What would it be like to feel that way again? So filled with utter and complete love?

"Are you alright?" Cort asked, genuinely concerned.

He couldn't speak. He could only nod and clear his throat against the uncomfortable tightening until he found his voice. Even then, it sounded thin and reedy.

"I don't know what came over me." Ben took a swallow of cider to ease his throat as he watched Moira pass the baby carefully to Maggie and show her how to hold the infant's head, another dear scene.

Cort chuckled. "I do. You're seeing your family for the first time." Ben raised an eyebrow at the comment. Cort continued, "That's your family, man. Moira, the girls and you. The four of you are a unit, a place to build from."

"Build?" Ben furrowed his brow. "As in more children? I'm thirty-eight, Cort. Besides, I've promised Moira—"

"I know what you promised her," Cort scoffed. "Unpromise it. Things can change between people. You are no longer strangers to one another. Perhaps such a promise isn't a promise as much as it is a penalty, an unwanted limitation now."

He didn't want to argue with Cort. It wasn't as simple to just "unpromise" it. Such a decision came with other feelings, other promises. It could not be undertaken lightly on his part. He would have to open his heart to love again and all that came with it, the hurt, the risk of loss along with the pleasure and joy of being fully known to another. It was a lot to ask of a man.

Moira took the infant back from Maggie and caught him staring from a distance. She smiled at him and raised an inquiring brow, thinking it was time to go.

"I do like watching her with the babe," he admitted to Cort with a nudge of his elbow. Another child, a child with Moira. The thought was not displeasing now that the feeling of viscera had receded. Perhaps in the future. There was much to be decided before he could give full vent to the possibility. He passed his tankard to Cort with a wink. "I need to go fetch my wife. I promised her a turn about the market." *My wife.* He was starting to like the sound of that.

The market was a brilliant collection of sounds and color as they strolled through. Ben had not dared let Moira come on her own. They were clearly marked as foreigners and perceived as people with money. Vendors flocked to them, pressing close and waving their wares with persistent intent. He kept a tight grip on Moira's arm and on occasion had to insist they be left alone.

Moira took the market in good stride, laughing at the monkey that sat on one man's shoulder and the bright-feathered parrot that squawked profanities from a cage for coins. Deeper into the market, the vendors let them go and they were free to wander. Still, he liked the feel of her arm through his and he was reluctant to release her for rather selfish reasons than concerns for safety.

"Look, oranges. We should take some back for the girls and as a gift for the quartermaster's wife for letting them stay with her," Moira suggested. The girls had been thrilled to have an afternoon on another ship and a chance to play with the baby. "We'll save the rest for Christmas presents," Moira decided. She was most taken with the variety fruits. "Limes and lemons, too, just look at this!"

Ben was pleased to hand over coins in exchange for a bag of fruits. He bought an extra orange and looked about for a sugar vendor. Spying one, he took Moira by the hand and made his way toward it. "Come on, we need sugar to eat this orange properly." He bought a cone of sugar and led her to a quiet spot in the market under a shade of palm fronds.

"What are we doing?" Moira looked on in delight as he peeled the orange and took a section to dip in sugar. He held it up for her inspection.

"We're eating the most delightful treat ever, sugared orange slices." He offered her a handkerchief for the juicy slice. She reached for the orange.

"My turn." It took a moment for him to realize what she meant to do. She dipped a section in the sugar and put it to his lips, feeding him with a playful smile. "I think this might be the most wonderful afternoon ever." There was something honest and winsome about her today. Perhaps it was the genuine joy that shone in her face. "I can't believe that I am here, somewhere near the equator, enjoying a summer day in the middle of December, walking in a market that is full of bright fruit and things I've never seen, eating oranges with you. I never thought I'd get to see a place like this." Her exuberance was positively intoxicating. "I feel…" She searched for a word. "Alive. That's it. I feel alive."

He did, too. Alive in all ways, as if eating oranges with this woman here in the market was the pinnacle of happiness. He moved toward her, touching his lips to hers. Then he suddenly realized what he'd done.

"I'm sorry, I should not have." Ben pulled away, but it was too late.

"Why not? Why should you not have?" Moira's hands gripped his coat, her eyes searching his. "I didn't mind." She whispered the confession. He felt her gaze study him for a long moment. "But you did. You minded."

Some of the joy leached out of the afternoon. He'd regret that kiss if it ruined the day. Things had been going so well and then Cort had put all sorts of ideas into his head and his imagination had run away with itself.

"What is it, Ben?"

He needed to explain, needed to find the words.

"You haven't let go of your wife yet, have you?" He wanted to protest that she was his wife, but Moira had the right of it and he could not lie to her.

"I loved Sarah for a long time," he said quietly amid the hubbub of the market.

Sarah. Her name. Spoken out loud at last. If he said nothing else, Moira would take that one word as a victory. They had grown closer over the last week since their truce. Ben had taken their new arrangement to heart. He was trying to let her in. They talked of the men, of his work, but still, so little of their conversations were about him, about his past. It was as if by not speaking of it, he could erase its existence, its impact on his life. But it was impacting his life and hers and what they could be together. Sarah was the ghost between them no matter how hard Ben tried to banish her.

"It's alright to say her name, Ben. It's alright to talk of her, to remember her." She knew all too well what that grief was like, of not knowing how to approach it, of wanting to ignore it. But ignoring it meant ignoring the people attached to it. Moira reached for his hand and interlaced her fingers through his.

"At first, my brother and I didn't talk of our parents. Then, we realized we wanted to, we needed to. That it was *right* to talk of them. They didn't need to disappear from our lives just because they were gone. Too many people made that mistake with us. After the funeral, people felt like it was inappropriate to mention them, like they were supposed to forget them. But that only made it worse." She paused, giving her mind time to sort through those early days and herself a moment to adjust to Ben's soft gaze on her. She was acutely aware he was listening intently to each word, searching for hope in them. She'd never been the source of hope to anyone before and it filled her with warmth, with gratitude, that he should seek out such assurance from her.

"Brandon and I had each other to talk to, to share memories with. You have the girls. I think they'd welcome stories of their mother. *I* would welcome them," Moira said softly. "I am not in competition with her. I have told the girls I don't mean to replace her. I simply mean to be myself." It occurred to her that perhaps Ben needed to hear that as well, that she didn't want to replace Sarah.

"I want you and me to be 'us,' to be ourselves, to have *our* life. I don't want to be a copy of the life you had with Sarah." Would he understand what she meant? "But I think Sarah can have a place in that life with us." Was she making any sense?

Ben's knuckles skimmed her cheek in a soft gesture. "Yes, but first, I want to tell you, I think you're the bravest woman I've ever known."

She offered him a slice of orange and a slip of a smile. "Then commend my bravery, and tell me about her."

Chapter Thirteen

"Sarah was everything I aspired to in my youth."
With the first words, it was as if the chains on his
heart had fallen away. "She was lovely and kind, always helping at the church, always helping with the
children at gatherings." He smiled in reminiscence—
perhaps for the first time since Sarah had died.

"She made the best apple pie." He laughed. "That
might have been the first thing I noticed about her.
A fifteen-year-old boy is always hungry." That had
been the year everything had changed between them.
"I'd known Sarah all my life. We were neighbors,
but that year we looked upon each other differently."

What a heady time that had been, falling in love
and experiencing all the feelings that went with it.
"We were too young to marry but we made plans,
so many plans." That had been heady, too, mapping
out one's life and dreams with another and know-

ing they cared for those dreams with the same reverence you did.

"We married as soon as I graduated from West Point. She was by my side as we slogged out to Fort Brady." She'd made a home for them in the rustic backwoods of Sault Ste. Marie, never complaining, always having a hot meal on the table for him, always having his clothes pressed and ready, was always happy to welcome him home each night.

"She sounds like a paragon," Moira said gently when he finished. There was no sign of jealousy or that he'd said too much, shared too much, despite her invitation that he do so. There was only acceptance and appreciation in her soft tone. In that moment, Ben thought Moira might be the paragon. It was a rare person who could listen to praise of one's predecessor without envy.

He was surprised to see that the sun had moved while he spoke. The hot market was cooling, the vendors beginning to pack up their stalls. He'd spoken far longer than he'd thought but it had felt good, so good, to share Sarah with someone, to try to explain what those years with her had been like, to show someone what he'd lost.

"Thank you for sharing. She sounds wonderful." Moira drew a breath and said in the same quiet tone, "I'm not her, Ben. I will never be her." There was a caution in that for him. Ben chose his next words carefully.

"I don't expect you to be, nor do I want you to be. You will be something altogether different." Perhaps that had been an unconscious reason he'd chosen Moira from among the girls at the party. She was the least like Sarah. She was reckless, confident to the point of brashness. There wasn't a particularly modest bone in her body, but there were honest ones. He'd seen that when she'd challenged Edward Brant. It had eaten at her to let a lie stand. But she was like Sarah in ways that mattered, ways that lay beneath the surface of her pretty face. She was fierce. Moira would fight for the people and causes she loved. It was sometimes an inconvenient talent when she turned that fierceness on him, something Sarah would never have done. Then again, there'd been no discord between them, no reason to quarrel.

"Thank you, Moira, for listening." No matter how gracious her offer, it could not have been easy for her. She'd seen how unlike Sarah she was. She might not think the contrast did her any favors. He would not have her thinking she was the lesser of the two. That had not been his point.

"I will listen, any time," she assured him but he knew better than to overburden her with his memories. Building a life together based on the new shared experiences of the Southern Hemisphere was one thing but building that life on the memories of a dead woman had the potential to be unhealthy. She stood up, brushing at her skirts. "It's getting late. We should head back to the ship." Tomorrow they would sail away, back to the journey.

They walked through the closing market slowly, this time with their arms about each other. Two friends, perhaps? Moira seemed subdued. He hoped she was not regretting the conversation.

"I will never pass this way again, never see this market again," Moira said solemnly. "This was a once-in-a-lifetime kind of day."

"You don't think you'll sail back to New York on visits to your brother and then back to California?" Ben thought the idea odd.

"I might go overland next time. It's only three months by wagon, and who knows, with the way railroads are being built, there might be a railroad that runs coast to coast. My brother talks with men who think there might even be a chance of building a canal in Panama. Not tomorrow, of course, but within a decade or two."

"That would be a wondrous thing." Ben played with the idea in his mind. "Not only would it cut down transportation time, it would circumvent the need to sail around the Cape."

Moira looked up at him. "You're worried about that. I can hear it in your voice."

"I've studied the maps and read accounts, none of them good." Ben *was* worried. His men weren't trained sailors. He didn't want a storm to panic them. But he wouldn't pass that worry on to Moira. She'd taken on enough today. Instead, he wrapped his arm about her more tightly, liking the feel of her against his side as they walked. "We've been lucky so far. Perhaps our luck will hold."

They were silent for the duration of their walk to the dock. Today had been full of hope; hope for himself that he might actually be capable of healing, of hope for the future, hope for their relationship, and yet Ben had one more question that must be asked before they returned to the ship.

"Are you sure, Moira, about staying? A ship will return to New York. I can arrange for you to be on it, if you've changed your mind. It's not too late."

Moira flashed him one of her teasing smiles. "And give up the chance to eat sugared oranges in exotic locales? Not a chance, Ben. Not a chance."

Moira wished she felt as brave as her words. The day lingered with her as she helped the girls make ready for bed. Lizzie sat before her, squirming a bit as she braided the younger girl's hair. Both had been delighted by the gift of oranges after supper tonight, declaring them the perfect end to a perfect day spent playing with baby Alta.

The day *had* been perfect for her, too. The baptism party had been a welcome relief to days of sameness and solitude. She and Ben had spent real time together, perhaps for the first time. They'd certainly talked of real things. He had revealed a piece of himself today in the sharing of his life with Sarah. She treasured that glimpse of him as a young man as much as that glimpse gave her pause. She tied a bit of ribbon around Lizzie's braid and started on the other one.

She would never be Sarah or even Sarah-like. She couldn't bake a pie, let alone prepare a meal. It wasn't an issue now when the ship's cook saw to all the food but it would be an issue in California when they had their own house. She'd listened with a dawning realization and growing trepidation today as the women at the baptism had exchanged recipes and housekeeping tips. She didn't know how to get a stain out of a shirt beyond the magical properties of hot water. But these women were marvels. They knew when to use salt or white vinegar. They knew how to turn the meanest of morsels into meals. Sarah had known those things, too. The comparison rose again unbidden.

Moira knew how to be a society wife: how to set a table, how to design a pleasant menu and seating chart, whom to order the best floral arrangements from, who had the best fish. She knew about fashion and a bit about sewing, enough to mend clothes, let down hems and do alterations. That reminded her: she needed to let down the hem in Lizzie's dress. The girl had grown an inch and a half since they'd left New York. Perhaps she even knew enough of sewing to manage making clothes. But beyond that, her housekeeping training had been vastly different from these women's, and the redoubtable Sarah. Did Ben realize that? Would he be disappointed in her when he discovered she didn't know the first thing about cooking? She'd have to learn. They couldn't live on oranges and kisses forever.

Moira felt her face flush at the thought of their day in the market. This had been a dangerous direction for her thoughts to take, especially when she'd discovered she *liked* kissing Ben. Today, she'd felt alive, being with Ben not unlike the way she felt when competing; racing her horse, or shooting her pistol, or the experiencing the thrill of flying across a dance floor with a skilled partner. Coming alive, that's what the thrill was and he brought it out in her.

How fascinating that Ben held the match to that particular spark. It prompted a host of other questions as to what that might mean for their marriage. Ben had been clear that he wanted a helpmate, perhaps in time a friend. It was clear from his stories today as well that he'd already experienced a great love in his life. Would he ever entertain finding such a love again? *With her?*

"Moira, do you love Father?" Maggie's question came from the bunk where she sat brushing her hair. Moira blushed. Surely, Maggie hadn't guessed the direction of her thoughts! How mortifying if she did. Moira had not meant to daydream or at least not to be transparent about it.

"Of course she does," Lizzie piped up, before Moira could gather her thoughts into a semblance of an answer. Lizzie wrapped her arms about herself in a dramatic hug. "It was a whirlwind romance! Love at first sight! He saw her at a house party and he *knew* she was the one!" Lizzie sounded like the newspaper boys who stood on New York street corners crying out the headlines to garner interest.

Maggie screwed up her face in thought. "But Moira can't be 'the one' because Father loved Mother. She was 'the one,'" Maggie insisted. She cocked her head and studied Moira. "You can't have two 'the ones,' can you, Moira? And how do you know? The world is full of a billion people and we will meet just a handful of them. What if we never meet 'the one'?"

Clearly, Maggie had given the issue a lot of thought. Moira would have to answer carefully, even as a certain warm thrill ran through her that Maggie would trust her for an answer. It was a sign of how far her relationship with the girls had come. She thought of what her own mother had said to her once when she was only a little younger than Lizzie.

"My mother told me that God didn't create one single person for us to love, but that love between a husband and wife grows over time, through sharing the joys and sadness of life. We shouldn't worry about looking for *the* right person." Moira hadn't thought about that piece of wisdom for a long time. Mostly because she'd refused to think of marrying. Marrying was for traditional girls. She'd been too busy rebelling against fate, against a God who hadn't answered a little girl's prayers.

She smiled at Lizzie. "That would be a disappointing expense of energy, don't you think? Spending all that time looking for perfection when we know full well perfection is not attainable."

Lizzie nodded, wide-eyed with interest. "What did your mother say we should do instead?"

"We should look for a good person who thinks as we do, feels as we do and all else will follow." After that kiss in the market, her own marriage seemed to shine in a new light. She recalled what Brandon had told her about Ben that first day, that he was a man of faith, a good man. It might have been all Brandon had known of him but it had been enough. She and Brandon had been raised in a faithful household, never mind that she'd done her best to stray from those foundations the older she got. Was it possible that Brandon had seen the potential between her and Ben because of Ben's faith?

Lizzie nodded, still pondering the idea of not looking for a singular right person and seeming to like the concept. "What a relief, then. It would have been terrible if Father was your 'one' but Mother was Father's 'one.'" She collapsed back against Moira in a dramatic flop worthy of the stage. "What a *tragedy* that would have been. You would have roamed the world with unrequited love." They'd obviously been reading Shakespeare that week and Lizzie was proudly trying out her new words. Lizzie could not imagine anyone not loving her father. Moira understood that dedication. She'd loved her father, admired and idolized him as the greatest man who'd ever lived at Lizzie's age. Then he'd died. She'd never had the opportunity to see that image tarnished.

Maggie met her gaze above Lizzie's head, ignoring her sister's dramatics. "I think Father would be difficult to love," she said thoughtfully. "His heart has been broken and I don't know if he can love in return. Someone might spend their love in vain." She paused and then added hesitantly, "Sometimes I wonder if he even still loves us."

Moira's heart cracked a bit at the girl's admission.

This was clearly something Maggie had pondered in her own heart, a great secret she'd kept bottled up. What did she say to that? She wouldn't give them lies or platitudes or false assurances she couldn't back up with proof. She hadn't been with the family long enough to be an authority on what Ben and the girls felt. But she had to say something. She didn't want Maggie taking her silence on the subject as affirmation of the girl's darkest thoughts. She opted for a question. "Why do you think that, Maggie?" she asked gently.

"Father keeps himself closed off because it hurts too much. Grandmother says that's why he left us with her. We remind him too much of Mother." Maggie fiddled with her hairbrush. "It's why he kept avoiding us even on the ship until you insisted he have dinner with us."

Lizzie looked up at her. "I like dinners so much better when Father comes. I think he's doing better," she offered hopefully to her sister.

"Your father does love you." The crack in Moira's heart widened for these two girls, who divined too much. Did Ben have any idea how much they guessed? Or how much they'd been told? She couldn't imagine he would let his grief remain center stage if it meant his daughters were suffering.

Maggie relented. "I know Father *wants* to love us, he's just not sure how. He's afraid to lose anyone again. It hurts to lose people when you love them." One didn't need to be grown up to know that or to know that sometimes it's not a matter of want. One did not always get to choose whom one loved or whom one lost or how much it would hurt.

Maggie's comment undid her. Moira had no words for them, nothing that would ease their hurt. Instead, she gathered the girls to her, an arm around each of them, and held them close. Then, slowly, very slowly, she felt their arms creep about her waist. Lizzie's first, and then Maggie's. Slowly, too, she felt gladness creep in, mingling with the sorrow and overcoming it; gladness that she'd not given up, gladness that she'd stayed and not thought for a moment about taking Ben's offer to return to New York. Finally, at last, perhaps her sorrow, her loss, had a purpose.

When the girls had fallen asleep, Moira took out writing implements and opened Reverend MacVickar's Bible to the family record pages at the back. The blank pages stared back at her, waiting for her, *begging* her to write on them. She lifted the pen and paused. Once written, the words could not be taken back. They would become the family history.

Moira wrote carefully *Benjamin Michael Shef-field married Sarah_____ on the _____ in the year _____*. She left blanks to be filled in later, but she would commemorate the girls' mother here. If today had been about anything, it had been about making Sarah a part of the family history. She was not to be erased. No one need to pretend for her sake that the beloved woman had never existed. Her pen moved on, noting the birth of each of the girls, again leaving the dates empty. Then she filled in her wedding to Ben. *September 24, 1846.* There were lines below that to list children.

She set the pen aside with a pang of sadness. She'd liked holding little Alta today. Babies had never intimidated her, but she'd never spent much time contemplating babies of her own any more than she'd spent time contemplating marriage. The conditions of her marriage wouldn't allow for children and perhaps Ben didn't want any more. He had two already.

She laughed at herself. One kiss in the marketplace, and she was starting to play a dangerous game of what if. What if Ben opened his heart to love? What if Ben changed his mind about the nature of their marriage? Today had been a start; how much further could he go? How much further did she *want* him to go?

There were other frightening what-ifs as well. What if she opened her heart to him and he didn't want it? What if he couldn't truly move past the loss of Sarah? What if Maggie was right and there was only one person in the world for you? And what if that person had been Sarah for Ben? He would never be fully hers. Could she live with that? *But what if he's meant to be yours and you are meant to be his and you don't even try for fear of failing, for fear of the unknown?* came the whispered prompt of her reckless heart.

She thumbed through the Bible, coming to the verse about the fruits of the spirit. *The fruit of the spirit is love, joy, peace, patience, kindness, goodness, faithfulness, gentleness and self-control.* These came to her so unnaturally. She'd strived today to model these with Ben, to draw him out, to learn him, but in truth she saw little of herself reflected in the list.

Love had not been gentle with her or with Ben in the past. It had been tempestuous and fierce, wrecking them and putting them back together; a reckless woman, a reclusive man who hid behind a fortress of strength. Love was not being kind with her now as it tempted her with Ben. Did she dare take the chance? What choice did she have when the alternative was to bungle through life alone together? No, love was not gentle or kind, Moira thought. Love was a storm and it was daring her to ride it.

Chapter Fourteen

The weather changed as they rounded Tierra del Fuego accompanied by the Cape's infamous williwaw winds billowing the sails to taut capacity and waves rising against the gunwales. The weather should not have been a surprise, but Ben was not prepared for the ferocity or the suddenness as he looked to the cloud-crowded sky. Just half an hour ago, the sky had been blue in accordance with mid-summer expectations in the tropics.

Perhaps he might have noticed earlier if his head hadn't been in clouds of a different sort. More had changed in the time since leaving Rio than the weather. Even amid the prelude of a storm, the thought of those changes made him smile. He and Moira had continued to work toward a friendly marriage, centered on the girls and getting to know one another.

Moira was right. His family was happening before his eyes. He could continue to let grief and hurt keep him from that, or he could join in it and take his place as an active head of the household. He'd chosen the latter and his heart had lightened and his fears had eased. It felt good to give Lizzie piggyback rides around the deck, to stroll with Moira and the girls *en famille* after the evening meal.

He was coming alive again, feeling again, and it was like a thaw after winter. He owed Moira for that as well. She didn't hide her feelings and he was learning from that. Her boldness was simply openness. He was learning, too, that such openness didn't come without risk. Moira was brave. It had been no small thing to utter the words *I didn't mind* in Rio when he'd kissed her. Those three words told him so much; that here was an opening, an opportunity to change the trajectory of their relationship, that although she'd made the overture with her words, she would take her cue from him in that regard.

He'd shared with her about Sarah and he had opened, just a little. It had felt good to have a confidante, someone he could share with. What more could he have, could *they* have, if he continued to share with her?

It would be the beginning of real relationship, one where there was mutual trust and faith in each other if he would take the next step. It was not a step to be rushed into, he knew. There would be no going back from it, no retreating, and yet such a relationship was a potent invitation that lingered, still beckoning to him weeks after they'd left Rio.

The ship pitched sharply to the right and Ben grabbed at the rigging to steady himself. The wind was coming up fast. He scanned the deck; surely Moira and the girls weren't still out here for lessons? Another gusting williwaw swept the deck, sending a crate skidding to the other side, narrowly missing an inattentive soldier. Ben leaped into action as the rain began. He yelled orders above the wind. "Tie down anything that's loose! That includes yourselves!" He moved from man to man giving the same instructions. "Make yourself a leash from the rope, tether it to the ship, or you'll wash overboard."

A dark head emerged on the quarterdeck and Ben squinted against the sheeting rain to make out the form, hoping his eyes betrayed him. They didn't. Fear pierced him. Moira was up here! He struggled toward her, fighting the wind and the pitch of the ship and deck made slippery from the water spilling over the side.

A large wave hit the ship and fear gripped him anew as he watched Moira slip, fall and slide across the deck until her hands caught hold of the quarterdeck railing. His heart raced. It had been too close and she was still down, unable to rise. Another roll of the ship, another errant wave cresting the gunwales would find her vulnerable. If she went over... He pushed the thought aside. He could not be paralyzed by fear now, not now when there was a chance for so much between them, not now when he was starting to live again.

"Moira! Hold on!" He was half crawling by the

time he reached her side. He got an arm about her waist and hauled her to him, taking a moment to hold her close and assure himself she was safe. He got them to their feet and dragged them both belowdecks where the pitching ship threw them against one another in the narrow corridor. She was soaked to the skin and trembling. For once, Moira had the good sense to be afraid.

"What in the world were you doing up here?" His words came out in a rasp, his breathing coming hard as he pushed wet strands of hair out of her face.

"I needed tea for Lizzie. She's got a bit of a stomachache." Moira lost her balance and clutched at his coat, her gaze moving over his shoulder as water gushed down the stairs leading abovedecks. Worry flashed in her gray eyes. "How bad is the storm?"

"It's the Cape," Ben offered with an air of assurance he hoped she found believable. "Ships are made to withstand such weather." He gave her a smile. "It's us you have to worry about." He meant it as a joke and then sobered when Moira didn't laugh. He ran his hands down the soaked arms of her gown. "Change your clothes, stay down here until I say otherwise. This too shall pass."

He might have succeeded in convincing her of that if the cry hadn't gone up: man overboard.

Moira paled. He didn't want to leave her but his men needed him. "Moira, I have to go," he began. He felt her hands uncurl from his coat as she gathered herself.

"Yes, go, we'll be fine down here." Moira managed the words. He could see her summoning her courage, and his heart moved even as he turned and took the stairs to the deck. The press of her hand on his arm stalled him for a brief moment, long enough for her to say, "Take care up there, Ben."

Their eyes caught, her gray gaze filled with unspoken messages: *Don't give us another thought, the girls are safe with me, I need you to come back.* His heart was too full to give her anything but a nod. Moira, who needed no one, who didn't care what anyone thought, needed him. And, he realized, he needed her. But what an inconvenient time to discover it.

She did not want him going up there, back into the storm, back into danger. She wanted him to stay with her, to comfort her, to assure her. She knew it was selfish. His men needed him. He could not be distracted by one woman. This storm was like nothing she'd ever experienced. Neither was the helplessness that went with it, at least not as an adult. She'd felt like this before when her parents had died. There'd been nothing she could do then to change that and there was nothing she could do now. She could not right the ship; she could not calm the storm.

You could pray, came the whispered thought. *God can calm the storm. God can right the ship.* If He wanted to, if He was listening. He'd not listened to her for a long time.

"Moira, did you get the tea for Lizzie?" Maggie peeked out of the cabin.

Moira straightened. She couldn't stop the storm but the girls were counting on her. She turned to face Maggie with what she hoped was a calm countenance. "No," She managed a laugh and gestured to her wet clothes. "The storm was too much. Don't worry, we'll think of something else."

"Good, because I think she's worse," Maggie said worriedly.

Moira quickly changed into a dry gown and apron and studied her patient. Lizzie was indeed worse. She was throwing up at regular intervals but more concerning was that Lizzie had developed a fever. "Well, I suppose a fever rules out basic seasickness." Moira smiled at Lizzie and tucked another blanket about the shivering girl. Lizzie's color wasn't good, either. She was pale and slightly green and she hadn't eaten since dinner the prior night. She was also struggling to keep even water down. That was worrying. Dehydration could set in.

"What do you think is wrong with her?" Maggie asked quietly at Moira's side.

"Am I going to die? Mama died from a fever." Lizzie gave a miserable little moan and Maggie looked positively terrified for her little sister.

"No, absolutely not. You're going to be uncomfortable for a little while, but you are going to get well," Moira said with all the matter-of-fact conviction she could muster.

The girls looked at her expectantly. They needed action; they needed her to take charge. She had to do something. But what? Other than helping Gemma nurse Ethan through a few bouts of colic, she'd not confronted illness directly. Too bad the physician who'd sailed with the fleet was on one of the other ships. With the storm, there was no way to reach him. She was Lizzie's first and last line of defense.

"The first thing we must do is get your fever down, Lizzie. Maggie, there's a book in the trunk about medicines and such. Get it out and look up the section on reducing fevers. Also, look for a bottle of peppermint extract. I don't know why I didn't think of it earlier. Peppermint can settle the stomach. We used it for my nephew. I think my sister in-law packed some."

"I found it!" Maggie held up the bottle and Moira felt a rush of gratitude toward Gemma's foresight. She mixed a dose into a cup of water for Lizzie and held it to her lips.

An hour later, Moira wished she could calm the sea as easily as she'd calmed Lizzie's stomach. But the storm apparently had worsened and while Lizzie's stomach seemed to be at tenuous peace with her, she was still unable to hold anything down and her fever continued to climb.

"I think she's better," Maggie ventured, looking for assurances.

Moira nodded and took a freshly wetted rag from Maggie. "Her stomach is better." She wouldn't worry Maggie with her own concerns. High fevers were dangerous and Lizzie was already weak from lack of food and liquid. At least for the moment, Lizzie was sleeping. She'd like to sleep through the storm as well.

"How long will the storm last?" Maggie asked as the ship gave a particularly perilous pitch.

"I don't know." Moira sat back, taking a break from nursing Lizzie. "Your father says rough seas are a product of the Atlantic and Pacific oceans meeting." She tried to be positive.

"Is Father safe up there?"

She hoped so. But how could anyone be safe amid this storm? She'd been on deck for just moments and nearly been washed away. "He was instructing all the men to lash themselves to something and to tie everything down. He knows what to do." *Please know what to do, please don't take any unnecessary chances,* she wished selfishly. But that wasn't the sort of man Ben was. That scared her more than the storm.

"Moira, maybe we should pray. Mama used to say that when we feel we are at our weakest we should pray the most." It was the first time Maggie had ever spoken about her mother or shared a memory with her. It was a sign of how worried Maggie must be. "After all," Maggie added, "Jesus calmed the sea for the disciples."

God hadn't for Jonah, Moira thought uncharitably. He hadn't calmed any proverbial seas for her, either. Still, she couldn't disappoint Maggie after such a tender overture. "Yes, why don't we." It was a big prayer: cure Lizzie, calm the sea, deliver them safe to California, keep Ben safe.

Two hours later, Moira decided God wasn't in a hurry. The storm persisted. Four hours later, Moira decided God still wasn't listening to her. Not only did the storm rage but Lizzie's fever did as well. The little girl was burning to the touch and had begun mumbling—a sign Moira feared of deliriousness. She threw back the covers and began rubbing Lizzie's feet with hard vigorous strokes to draw the fever down. It was the only thing she hadn't tried yet. She was fast running out of options.

That was how Ben found her when he blew into the cabin shortly before midnight, drenched and dripping. It had been hours since he'd checked on them, knowing they were safe belowdeck. He was instantly concerned for his daughter. "How is she?" Ben's brow furrowed with worry at the sight of Lizzie. "This is more than a stomachache. She must have eaten something. There are men sick as well." Ben knelt swiftly beside the bunk and pressed a cold hand to his daughter's cheek. It felt good to have Ben here, someone to share the burden with.

"Is it a disease? Something contagious?" Moira was worried now that she should have sent Maggie to Ben's cabin sooner. Maggie was there now, sleeping.

Ben shook his head, water droplets falling on the blankets. "I don't think so. I'd guess it was something wrong with the meat last night. Not all the meat, obviously. You and I and Maggie and many of the men are quite fine. Eating bad food can engender a fever as well as stomach upset."

"I gave her peppermint for her stomach and it

seemed to help but I can't get the fever down. It keeps rising." A look passed between them, words unspoken. Rising fevers were deadly. They were swift and ravaging and Lizzie had little in reserve with which to fight it. Fear flashed in Ben's eyes. He was no stranger to this. He'd walked this way before. Moira could only imagine what must be going through his mind: to lose his wife, to lose his daughter in the same way.

He murmured encouragement to Lizzie, dropping a kiss on her hot forehead. "Get well, Lizzie, you'll want to see the porpoises after the storm passes. Papa is helping to keep the ship righted so that we all come through safely." Moira had never heard him or the girls refer to him as Papa. It always had been more formally Father. But he was definitely "Papa" in these precious moments. Such tenderness, such care awoke the angry warrior in her. Ben should not have to endure so much.

She put a hand on his shoulder as he talked to a listless Lizzie. "We won't lose her, Ben." Not on her watch. The fierceness in Moira gave her strength. She would personally face down death if it came to call tonight. She would do it for this little girl and for this man, both of whom had claimed her heart.

Ben rose, careful not to lose his balance. His gaze was serious. "We must pray, Moira. For the ship, for Lizzie. It will be a long night." She could see the worst in his eyes. Part of her would have liked a little less honesty. She didn't dare take the last of his hope and tell him she already had. She merely nodded as he slipped out the door. If God wasn't going to work a miracle tonight for Lizzie, then she would.

Lord, save my daughter, roll back the storm. We are at Your mercy. Without that mercy, they were lost. The mainmast creaked dangerously with each gust. If it fell, disaster was imminent. Ben's litany ran through his mind during the long night as he worked tirelessly with the captain to keep the ship safe, the men safe, their supplies safe. It was a humble man's prayer, a "sun stand still" prayer for the impossible, for things beyond a man's power and control.

Just as Joshua had prayed for the sun to stand still on the day of battle, Ben prayed for Lizzie and for the ship, and for Moira, that she have the strength to believe. He'd not missed the flicker of defiant doubt in her eyes. "She doesn't think You'll answer, Lord. Show her she's wrong. Show her she's not forgotten." Even as he prayed, even as he put his faith in God, Ben acknowledged he'd never been this afraid of losing everything he loved in his entire life.

Chapter Fifteen

Ben went below shortly before dawn, desperate to see how Lizzie was faring. He knew too well how precarious these dark hours were for the seriously ill. The storm was beginning to abate. He could do no more on deck but perhaps he could help Lizzie, could help Moira. Half his prayer was answered. The storm would blow itself out by full morning. Thank You, Lord, for delivering us. He breathed the quick words of gratitude. Now, there was Lizzie to get through.

He entered the cabin silently. The scene before him would have been touching if the circumstances weren't so dire. Lizzie lay sleeping the restless sleep of the fevered, her face flushed, a rag across her forehead. Moira slept beside the bed, her head on Lizzie's feet, her arms outstretched. What a night Moira'd had and her fight still wasn't done. *Their* fight. Lizzie was going to get well. He couldn't allow himself to believe otherwise.

Ben knelt at Lizzie's head, touching her cheeks and smoothing her hair back. Her skin was so hot and it had been for a long time now. The last twelve hours felt like a lifetime. She gave a little moan in her sleep. "Hush, Lizzie. Papa's here," he whispered. The rag on her forehead was warm. He took it and dipped it in the basin. "This will feel better."

Lizzie didn't even flinch against the coolness. He reached for her hand, so hot and small inside his own, and limp. Her pulse beat fast and shallow. That was not good. Panic rose. He could not lose her. He could not lose his daughter; it would be like losing Sarah all over again. In his gut, he knew it would be far worse to lose this sweet little girl whom he'd held when she'd taken her first breath. "No, Lord, not my Lizzie. Don't take her," he breathed. "Turn back the fever like You turned back the storm."

He stroked Lizzie's hand, trying to reach her. "Lizzie, don't you leave me. Who will I give piggyback rides to? Who will tell me silly jokes? Or teach me to balance a pencil on my lip? We should see porpoises any day now. I know how much you wanted to see them." He talked until he ran out of things to say and then he sang, the old lullabies Sarah had sung to the girls when they were little and she'd walked the floor with them at night.

"You have a beautiful voice." Moira's sleepy head rose from the bunk. "I'm sorry, I fell asleep. How is she?" She rooted around for a dry towel and passed it to him. In his haste to see Lizzie, he'd not taken time to dry off.

Ben shook his head. "I can't lose her, Moira. She and Maggie are the last I have of Sarah. I promised Sarah I would keep them safe."

"We won't lose her, Ben." Moira soothed him, her hand at his back as she knelt beside him, massaging the tight muscles of his neck. After a night of battling the storm, of looking after others, someone was looking after him. It was his undoing. He felt his shoulders begin to shake with weariness, with emotion.

"Sarah died in the dark hours. I barely arrived in time. I should have been there. I never should have left her. If I'd been there, perhaps she might have lived, perhaps she would not have taken ill in the first place, not have gone to nurse the sick, not have caught the fever. It took her fast, just like this fever."

He was vaguely aware that he was rambling now as Moira stroked his back, all the guilt he'd held in tight pouring out. "The doctor said she was waiting for me, that it wouldn't be long now. She would be gone before the sun." At the last, Sarah had been surprisingly lucid in the way dying people are, gathering their strength for one last moment in the world. *Take care of the girls. Keep them safe until we are together again.*

"What a poor job I've done of it, too." In his grief, he'd distanced himself from them, and now just when he'd opened himself back up, he stood to lose Lizzie. He'd held himself apart, to protect himself, to make himself strong, to make sure he was never hurt again. "I can't lose anyone else, Moira." His throat was choked with sobs. "We lost a man tonight. Drowned before we could reach him."

He was jumping subject to subject now, his mind a riot of thoughts and feelings. He reached for Moira's hand and held on to it tight, a lifeline of its own. "I almost lost you, too. When I saw you go down on the quarterdeck and the wave sweep through." He couldn't complete the thought. To lose Moira, to lose Lizzie, it was unfathomable.

"You didn't lose me. I'm right here," Her voice was firm and strong.

He raised his head and met her steady gray eyes. He'd once thought only his girls would benefit from the strength he saw in Moira. He'd not thought he would, too, that he would come to need her tenacity and her bold bravery for himself. *And you fool, you nearly let hurt and grief keep you from opening your heart,* came the scold. It gave him strength. He wasn't going to lose Lizzie, not when he'd come so close to reclaiming his life again, not when he needed Lizzie to be part of it. But he had no medicine, no magic cure. He had something better. "Will you pray with me, Moira?" He wasn't accustomed to asking for anything but her answer was swift as if it never occurred to her to deny him anything. The thought of having her beside him in this crisis, supporting him without question filled him with renewed strength, a reminder of how much he'd come to rely on her in the weeks since they'd left New York. A reminder, too, of how much she'd come to mean to him.

"Of course," she replied softly. "But you should

know, God isn't in the habit of answering my prayers," she warned bleakly.

Ben smiled. "You don't know that, Moira. He always answers, just not in ways we recognize or understand perhaps until later, much later, even when it seems that happiness can only exist if there's sadness. The Lord who is quieting the storm, who brought us through the night, can save Lizzie."

"How do you do it, Ben? How do you keep believing in the face of adversity? Your wife is dead, your child is desperately ill, we were nearly drowned and shipwrecked, and yet you believe without doubt," Moira whispered. "I've had to believe in me. That's all I've felt I can rely on."

He squeezed her hand. "And the Lord, Moira. You can rely on Him always. He has not forsaken you. He has brought you here for a reason. We are together for a reason." She'd already done so much for him, brought so much back to his life. He wanted to do this one thing for her, to show her that she was not alone, that God had not deserted her, just as God had not deserted him not even in his darkest hours. God would not desert them now. He bent his head and began to pray. *Save Lizzie. Help Moira to believe, to open her heart to You as she's opened my heart to her, to the possibility of loving again and all that goes with it.*

Ben did not know how long they knelt in prayer, only that Moira stayed beside him, her own head bowed, her hand clasped in his as they gave strength to one another. At some point a little voice broke the silence with a single word. "Papa?"

His eyes flew open and Moira started beside him. Lizzie was awake. He reached out a hand to her cheek. "Moira, I think her fever's broken. Lizzie, how do you feel?" Relief surged through him followed by jubilation. *Thank You, Lord. Thank You, Lord.*

"I'm hungry."

Ben rose, stiff from kneeling. "I'll see to getting some broth from the galley." The storm had calmed to choppy seas. He could navigate the distance safely. "I'll bring breakfast for all of us," he said, bending swiftly to place a kiss on Lizzie's forehead.

The storm was over and they'd come through, all of them, and there was joy on the other side. He was going to make the most of it.

With Lizzie's recovery assured, Moira made the most of Christmas on board the *Loo Choo*. The storm had been a sobering reminder of the dangers they all faced. There was the loss of their comrade to mourn and a ship to repair. But it was also time to celebrate having coming this far. Christmas provided a chance to turn the page on their grief and look ahead. She planned a pantomime for Christmas Day and conspired with Cook for plum duff as a special dessert for the men. She had presents planned for the girls—oranges from Rio and the hair ribbons from Stewart's. She could hardly wait to see their faces. But the best surprise was one she couldn't plan—the snowfall that lightly coated the deck while porpoises and dolphins cavorted off the gunwales.

"It's like a Christmas miracle all its own," she confessed to Ben as they enjoyed the snowfall on deck, bundled up in coats they hadn't worn since the ship had passed the equator. Most of the men had elected to stay below. The waters were still choppy and the weather was frigid. But the girls were enchanted with the porpoises and dolphins. They stood watching the animals, their new ribbons in their hair, a little farther down the railing.

"I don't think I'll take Lizzie's energy for granted again." Moira smiled watching the girl throw bread crumbs to a wheeling gull. She paused, aware of Ben's silence as he studied his girls. "Are you upset about the hair ribbons?" she asked cautiously.

He laughed down at her, his eyes crinkling at the corners. "No, whyever would you think that?"

"You were so adamantly against them the day the girls saw them at Stewart's. You thought them frivolous," Moira reminded him. "They were the reason I was late for the wedding and I went against your orders. You said no and I decided I liked yes better."

Ben was thoughtful for a moment. "You argued with me that day in Stewart's. You had me wondering what I'd gotten myself into."

"And do you still wonder?" Despite the growing tenderness between them since the night of the storm, Ben had made no move to kiss her, although they'd certainly furthered their relationship in ways that some might find far more meaningful.

"I wonder how I was so lucky, Moira. You've been all that the girls and I have needed even when we didn't know better ourselves." He raised her hand to his lips and kissed her cold knuckles. "You saved me from myself. You forced me to see what no one else was willing to make me see—that I needed to make peace with the past, that I needed to set aside my fear and live again. I can only hope that I've done half as much for you."

His words touched her. It was hard to believe she'd done all that simply by being herself. "You took me out of New York. You gave me a chance to find myself, just as you promised."

He grinned. "I am a man of my word."

She reached into her coat pocket and took out a small, square package wrapped in brown paper. "I have a present for you."

Something warm twinkled in his eyes. "You do? I didn't expect anything." He undid the string to reveal the carefully pressed and embroidered handkerchiefs within. His thumb traced the initials. "You did these? They're wonderful. Thank you, Moira." The air about them charged, a bolt of awareness leaping between them. Moira licked her lips.

Ben's blue eyes lingered on her face. A trill of excitement raced through her. They were building something here between them, building toward the hope of realizing the friendship he'd spoken of in New York and perhaps even beyond that.

Moira smiled as his hand cradled her jaw and his mouth captured hers in a Christmas kiss.

"I told you they loved each other."

Lizzie's smug whisper broke the enchantment and Moira blushed furiously over being caught. Ben stepped back from her and she flashed a look in his direction. How had he taken the words? Was he embarrassed? He was certainly uncomfortable. Because of the kiss? Or because of the use of the word *love*? A little trickle of fear ran through her. Would he disavow Lizzie's words? Deny them? Moira hoped not. Even if it wasn't true, the girl would be devastated and it would lfuel Maggie's belief that her father was beyond love. Sometimes it was simply best to say nothing.

Ben seemed to agree. He cleared his throat and turned his rather flustered attention to the girls. "What is it that you want?" he said kindly. "Are you ready to go down below?"

Maggie stepped forward, taking her sister's hand a little nervously. "We didn't mean to interrupt. We just wanted to say thank you for the hair bows. We'll save them for special occasions."

"You're very welcome." Moira looked from one girl to the next, sensing there was more on their minds, something yet to be said.

"There's one more thing," Maggie stammered shyly. "Lizzie and I have been talking. Do you remember when you said we could discuss what to call you? We settled on Moira but we think we would like to call you Mama Moira if that would be alright with you? And with you, Father? If you don't think it would be disrespectful to Mother?" Maggie and Lizzie had clearly put a lot of consideration into the request.

Moira glanced at Ben as he knelt before the girls, an arm around Lizzie. "I think your mother would like that very much. She'd want you to welcome Moira." How had she ever thought him a stoic, passionless man? Here was a far different man from the man she'd encountered at the Bostwick house party, a man who'd been waiting to be revealed, to be set free.

"I'd be honored if you called me Mama Moira," she assured them.

Ben took her hand, completing the little circle he made with the girls. "What a Christmas this is turning out to be. We have so much to be thankful for. Lizzie's good health, our safe passage and the chance to be a real family again. It's one for the record books, for sure."

Moira smiled, an idea coming to her. "Speaking of record books, why don't we go to the cabin and fill in the pages of the Bible. I have your names but I need your birth dates for the family tree." It seemed the perfect way to end Christmas Day, a day that celebrated a family not unlike this new family she was part of. She was no more the mother to these girls than Joseph had been the father to the baby in the manger, and yet neither family was any the less for it.

A family. She hadn't known she'd wanted one, but now she wouldn't give it up for the world. When she glanced over her shoulder at Ben, the look on his face suggested he agreed and it warmed her in inexplicable and unexpected ways to be in accord this man.

Chapter Sixteen

March 22, 1847

The family gathered at the rail as San Francisco harbor came into view, Ben's chest swelling with pride and happiness. They'd made it. Seventeen thousand miles across an ocean.

He glanced at Moira standing beside him, the ribbons of her hat fluttering in the wind. What a journey it had been, not only of miles but of emotional distances as well. They were not the same two strangers who had pledged themselves to one another in New York. They were both changed, he thought, and from his perspective, for the better. He was a better man, a better father, because of her. He looked forward to continuing that particular journey with her in the newly named Yerba Buena—it was San Francisco now, having changed while they were at sea. A message had come from Colonel Stevenson, whose ship had arrived earlier than the *Loo Choo*, that the town had been renamed in January. As surprises went, the name change was minor.

Since leaving the treacherous Cape waters behind, the rest of the voyage had been accomplished with only a few difficulties. The *Loo Choo* and the *Susan Drew* had opted to put in at Valparaiso for water and to regroup after the storm. It was a necessary decision but it had consequences of its own. Twenty-nine men, perhaps unnerved by the storm, had deserted in empty barrels, choosing instead to take their chances on land as new inhabitants of Chile instead of journeying on to California. The other episode that plagued them had been a bout with the doldrums. The *Susan Drew* had gotten through but the *Loo Choo* had lost the wind and sat idle in the tropics, which was why they were the last of the original three ships to arrive in San Francisco, ten days later than the *Susan Drew*.

"We made it," Moira whispered for him alone to hear. She squeezed his hand, the gesture hidden by the folds of her skirts. "You got us through. From high winds to no winds, from shore to shore, you've delivered us safely."

Her praise warmed him but he was an honest man. He had not done this alone. They'd gotten each other through. Especially in the second half of the voyage, they'd taken strength from each other; from the assurance of a touch to kind words at the end of the day that reminded them they weren't alone. And prayer. Prayer had gotten him through, prayers for guidance and prayers for thankfulness that God had seen fit to put Moira in his life.

Lizzie tugged at his hand. "Where's the town, Papa?"

"It should be coming into view any moment." The bay was enormous by Ben's standards. They'd passed an island and what was known as the Sausalito Port. There were American ships docked there and the men, thinking this was their final destination, had been confused when they sailed on past. "We're coming out of Yerba Buena Cove and the harbor should be, just over there."

"I see it!" Lizzie gasped as an American flag came into view, flying high over what had once been the Mexican barracks. A cheer went up behind Ben as the men crowded at the railings to see land and to see their new home.

"Is that all there is?" Maggie asked quietly after a while and Ben had to admit that she was only saying what he was thinking.

Still, he wished she hadn't asked it within earshot of his men. After the initial thrill of safe arrival, San Francisco failed to impress the weary traveler. From the deck of the ship, the town appeared to comprise a few framed buildings, adobe warehouses and a deserted barracks. In truth, the bay around the town looked busier and more active than the town. The bay was full of all kinds of ships from warships to storeships, a sign that the war was mopping up for America.

"Isn't it exciting, Maggie?" Ben answered carefully, favoring his family with a confident smile. "This is a new start for us. We can make this land as we'd like it. We couldn't do that if it was already done for us."

But even as he said the words, he was aware of the fallacies beneath them. His fresh start came at the expense of someone else being pushed off the land, an abstract concept he'd not dwelled on overmuch in New York, but seeing the flag flying over the empty barracks drove the reality home in a strong, poignant way. He was not a man who wanted his happiness made from the sacrifices and losses of others.

Shortly after they anchored, Ben called the men to form ranks to welcome aboard the two men who'd rowed out from the town, ostensibly as a greeting committee. One man was French, a Victor Prudhorn, and the other identified himself as a Californian by the name of Mariano Vallejo. He spoke Spanish, but Prudhorn had some English. Between Prudhorn's English and Ben's very good French and untried Spanish, they managed to have a useful conversation. Colonel Stevenson had taken his troops to the Presidio located above the straits. The *Loo Choo* men were to march out and join them. They could disembark by rowboat at Clark's Point and journey from there.

Ben met the instructions with some relief. His men would have actions to take that would keep their bodies and minds busy. There would be little time for them to be disappointed at the state of their destination at journey's end. After the visitors left, he called his officers to him and dispersed instructions. Today was to be spent packing and securing the ship. They would set off tomorrow. It would be no small undertaking, he had six hundred odd men and staffers to row ashore and march overland in some organized fashion, yet the thrill of the challenge hummed through his blood. He wondered what Moira would say. Would she be disappointed they had farther to go?

"So the end of the journey isn't the end of the journey." Moira leaned back on the railing, laughing when he discussed the day with her that night. Maggie and Lizzie were just beyond them at the rail, looking up at the stars. She and the girls had spent a busy day packing and helping out around the ship with various chores.

"Just tomorrow and then you can rest," he assured her. "Vallejo and Prudhorn had letters from Stevenson for us as well. Stevenson has been making the Presidio inhabitable." He gave her a quick smile. "Perhaps it works in our favor to have arrived late. The work of sweeping out will have been done for us. You can hang your curtains."

"Rest?" Moira laughed again. "There is no such thing as rest with you, Benjamin Sheffield. There's ships, and marches and moving from place to place. There will be unpacking." And a house to set up. Surely, she could do it. Just because she hadn't done it before didn't mean she couldn't do it. It would just be new.

"Are you worried about what we'll find at the Presidio?" Ben asked, watching her brow furrow, perhaps unconsciously. He could understand it if she was. Today's arrival had been visually disappointing. San Francisco was no New York. It looked more like a trading post than civilization.

Moira shook off her frown. "No, not at all. I've never moved before, you know. I've lived in the same house all my life. This will be a new adventure." She and Ben had moved to a good place in their relationship. She didn't want to ruin it with reminders that he'd married a society miss, not a pioneer woman who could live beyond the luxuries of town. She *would* learn, she vowed.

"You will do famously, Moira. There's nothing to it." Ben gathered her close and she let herself take refuge in the warmth of his body.

"It's a little bit disconcerting to think this is our last night aboard the ship." She breathed in the male scent of him, all strength and spice. "After days, even weeks of wanting this journey to be over, I find myself reluctant to leave. I think I might miss the *Loo Choo*." The ship had become a special place for her; it held memories. Even now, with equipment stowed and crates packed and stacked for disembarking, the ship had a ghostly quality to it, as if they'd already left.

"We'll have our own home, our own space at the Presidio. We'll make new memories," Ben murmured at her ear. "Will that please you, my wild Moira?"

She turned in his arms, her own going about his

neck with an ease that she'd not thought possible six months ago. "Am I so wild anymore?"

"I would never want you tamed, Moira. Who would tell me the truth?" Ben laughed and then sobered. "I've been happy these past weeks, Moira. Dare I hope you have been, too? You don't wish you'd gone back in Rio?"

She searched his face, his words catching her by surprise. How odd to think this man who commanded men, who'd brought them all this far, would doubt his appeal. She understood he was not just asking about happiness regarding her situation but her happiness with him uniquely. "No, of course not, Ben. I feel like I'm discovering myself for the first time, what I'm capable of, and what I want to be."

"And what is that, Moira?"

"A good wife to you, Ben, a woman you can be proud of. I want to be an advocate for women here so that this can be a place of new starts for them, too." She was aware that there were those who would find the two goals incompatible. How could an outspoken woman inherently be a good wife? The very definition precluded it. "I want Lizzie and Maggie to know they can be whatever they want to be, that the world we make will have a place for them. They don't have to change to please a man."

She'd changed but not to please Ben. She'd changed because she finally understood herself. She could be bold without challenging the Edward Brants of the world to pistol contests. Honesty was bold. Directness was brave. She needn't crave attention. While she'd not had a use for society's rules, she'd had a need for its attention as if to say look at me, I am still here. I am more than the poor orphaned heiress.

"All women?" Ben mused in the darkness, his blue eyes intent on her although she sensed his thoughts weren't entirely with her. There was something else floating in his mind.

"All women. Mexican women, Indian women, American women, all of us, Californians. We are not so different." Her words brought a smile to Ben's face. Whatever thought had momentarily drawn him away faded.

"Shall I see you to your cabin, Mrs. Sheffield? It will be an early day tomorrow and a long one. I hope you and the girls are prepared for walking."

Moira laughed. "It's not so long, only three miles. We've had six months to prepare for walking. I daresay our legs will rejoice in the opportunity."

Her legs were definitely not rejoicing at the end of the march the next day and there was still work to be done. The trek had involved hills, for one thing. Moira learned two additional lessons about moving with the army. First, that hauling things in wagons overland was slow work, and second, keeping six hundred men in a line was slow work as well. If walking three miles should have taken a little more than an hour for a normal person, the military could stretch it out to twice that long. They'd left the *Loo Choo* at dawn and arrived at the Presidio in the late morning with much of the day still ahead of them although it felt as if it should be night.

She and the girls saw Ben long enough for him to direct them to their "home," an adobe brick structure containing three crumbling rooms and two windows, and to leave two men with her to unload the wagon carrying their trunks. The house barely warranted the name, Moira thought.

Maggie looked as if she were about to cry. "This is it?" Maggie turned forlorn eyes her direction as if to say, we've traveled this far for this? Moira knew she was thinking of her grandmother's comfortable house in West Point, and her uncle's mansion with more rooms than he could use on Bleeker Street.

Moira slipped an arm around each of the girls, summoning strength from some heretofore untapped inner well, and smiled. "What a project this will be, making this into our home. Did you ever have a dollhouse? I had one that I could arrange any way I liked to my heart's content. This will be just like that, only when we're done, it will be our real house."

Maggie looked at her dubiously. The first of the trunks were hefted down from the wagon. Moira tried again. "It will be a bit like Christmas, opening the trunks and seeing what we packed six months ago. There will be all those things from Stewart's," she enthused, hoping she was convincing the girls.

"It will be a little like a second Christmas. I can't even remember everything I packed or bought. Maggie, you open the first trunk and take inventory while I tour the house." She thought it would be best to keep the girls busy while she saw the house first and perhaps had a chance to ward off any further disappointment.

Moira stepped into the adobe-bricked structure. And sighed. The inside wasn't much better but she was immediately thankful for small things like the dirty wood planking someone had laid down. The flooring could be swept. It could be covered with a rug, and it could have been worse. There could only have been a dirt floor. Benefits of being an officer's wife, she joked to herself.

The two windows had glass panes, another luxury she didn't dare take for granted, not after seeing the dilapidated state of the fort in general. There was a fireplace but no stove. That did give her trepidation. How was she to cook over a fire? Then again, how was she to cook at all? Beyond the common room were two smaller rooms meant to be bedchambers as evidenced by the bare iron bedsteads in each of them. Mentally, Moira ran through items from the trunks. Colorful quilts would brighten the rooms and there were curtains to hang after the windows were cleaned.

She strode outside to find the girls rummaging through the trunks, the excitement of exploring the house goods offsetting initial disappointment. "Good news, girls. We have floors, real floors." She handed a pail to Lizzie and a broom to Maggie. "Let's get started, we have a home to put together. Let's surprise your father with a proper welcome home tonight."

The afternoon sped by in a flurry of unpacking and activity. After months aboard ship living minimally, there was a certain joy in being surrounded by personal things. Hours later, Moira stepped back to survey the common room, the place where they would eat and gather as a family, the place where she might eventually entertain other ladies at the fort. This was the space that would be a kitchen, a dining room and a parlor for the family. There were only a few pieces of furniture—she had more than this in her bedroom alone on Elm Street—but here those five pieces seemed the height of luxury. They were pieces Ben must have packed. She'd never seen them before and it had been a pleasant surprise when the men had unloaded them.

The table with its chairs sat at the back of the room, in front of the credenza against the far wall. The credenza was a point of pride to Moira. She and the girls had carefully unwrapped the dishes that were displayed now on the shelves: creamware from England that had been part of her trousseau. She'd not picked it herself or been interested in it at the time. Gemma had ordered it years ago. She was glad for it now, as she was glad for the painted teacups and porcelain tea service that graced the credenza beside a decanter for Ben, already filled with cider. The table itself was covered in a white cloth they'd been given as a wedding gift, and a crystal vase stood proudly in the center, flanked by two silver candlesticks with real wax candles, another wedding gift. Tomorrow, maybe they would venture out for wildflowers for the vase.

A fire burned in the hearth. She'd talked one of the men into laying one before they left, and enough wood for the night was stacked beside it. The fire warmed the room and cast homey shadows as the last of the afternoon light filtered in through the front windows of the "parlor."

The settle and two chairs were set about the braided rug found at the bottom of a trunk and a tall secretary sat against the wall, its top half a glass-doored bookcase that now held the books Ben had packed and the school supplies she'd purchased for the girls. The bottom half was a cabinet with a door that folded down to reveal a writing desk. Letters could be written from there. White curtains adorned the windows, looped back with lengths of white cord.

Moira lit a lamp and placed it in the window with a sense of overwhelming pride as the girls came out of the bedroom they would share. They'd been making beds and folding clothes in the now-empty trunks that would be used in absence of a wardrobe while she'd busied herself in the front room. Although busy hands hadn't kept her mind from drifting to the bedroom situation. She and Ben would need to share a room for the first time. The idea did funny things to her belly. Might their marriage take on a new trajectory because of it?

"Well, girls, what do you think? Have we transformed the place?" Moira held the light up, showing off the front room.

Lizzie looked around at the completed project with wide eyes. "Oh yes, it's beautiful," she breathed. Moira thought so, too.

"Well, Maggie?" Moira asked hesitantly. Maggie had worked hard this afternoon and Moira knew how disappointed the girl had been at the outset. "What do you think?"

"I think it's wonderful," Maggie said at last, her voice trembling. "I'm sorry I doubted. I don't know how you do it, Mama Moira, making the most of things. I can't do it." A tear slid down her cheek. "I want to, I really do, but I can't. I miss my home. I miss all the pretty things. I know I shouldn't. I know it's frivolous. But I do."

Moira went to the girl and wrapped her arm about her. "Of course you do. It's only natural. And you're wrong, you can do it, just maybe not yet. You're only thirteen, Maggie. You have a lot of growing up to look forward to. It will come."

"What if it doesn't come?" Maggie's forlorn tone tore at her heart. Hadn't she once felt that way, too? She led the girls to the settle in the new "parlor" and knelt before them.

"It will come, Maggie," she said, taking her hand. "It already has. When I first met you I saw a girl who had become both a mother and a sister to her little sister, a girl who'd been forced to grow up a bit too soon. You spoke for Lizzie, you reminded Lizzie of the right things to do. You were quite the little mother, knowing exactly what your sister liked and what she needed." It had been rather intimidating.

"You mean I was bossy." Maggie sighed.

"No, you were trying to help her, trying to protect her as best you knew how. It was very noble, very self-sacrificing. Kindness and strength are already in you, Maggie." Maggie was truly starting to blossom, starting to come into her full potential. There was less of the petulant child Moira had met in New York about her these days and more of the caring young woman Moira hoped she'd become.

Moira rose and went to the newly filled bookshelves of the secretary. "Shall we have a story before Papa comes home?" The girls gathered around her as she sat back down between them. She opened the book and looked up for a moment to survey the parlor they'd made. This would be the first of many days reading from the settle, the girls with her in their new home. It wasn't Elm Street and nothing near as fine as the home Moira had grown up in, but she was proud of it and seeing Maggie and Lizzie here with her in this place filled her with a pleasant sense of contentment, of achievement. Maybe she could do this after all. She smiled at the girls and began to read.

Chapter Seventeen

The light in the window drew him home. *Home.* The word struck Ben anew with its sense of comfort and security. How odd it was to associate that word with a crumbling adobe structure that hadn't resembled anything habitable let alone a home when he'd left Moira and the girls there this afternoon. Home was not a word he'd used much in the last three years. He'd lost his home when Sarah died and not only physically, because home was not a place. Home was a person. People were what gave a home its comfort and security. Moira was that person for him. Moira was home, the girls were home.

He paused one last time before opening the door, steeling himself against an uncertain welcome. Would the girls be disappointed in their new abode? Would Moira be wishing she'd gone back to New York? Or that she'd never left? She'd assured him otherwise last night but that was before he'd made her walk three miles to a fort that offered not even the meanest of amenities, and that was after seeing the crude establishment that passed for the city of San Francisco. How much more disappointment could he ask her to shoulder? And the girls as well. The men had taken considerable cajoling today.

Ben pushed open the door and stepped inside. For the first time that day he was not beset with disappointed grumblings. Moira looked up from her book and the girls ran to him, even Maggie, who sometimes thought she was too old for such things.

Lizzie had him by the hand. "Do you like our house? Come and see what we've done! This is the parlor," Lizzie proudly announced, giving Ben a moment to sweep the little space, to note the furniture had made the journey intact. She dragged him forward toward the dining table. "See the credenza?" She tried out the new word with pride. "We put the dishes up."

He met Moira's gaze over Lizzie's head and smiled. He hoped that smile conveyed the gratitude he felt in this moment; how pleasant it was to come home and see his daughters happy, his home domestically delightful. He wanted to stare a while longer at the details—the tablecloth, the vase, the cookware lining the mantel of the fireplace, the braided rug in the "parlor"—but Lizzie wanted to show him the bedrooms.

"This bed is mine. I made it myself with the quilt from grandmother. Mama Moira says it will help us think of her when we snuggle in at night."

The girls' room was small, just enough room for the two single bedsteads with a trunk at each foot, presumably being used for clothes, Ben guessed, and a washstand in the corner, adorned with an ewer and basin Ben remembered Moira selecting at Stewart's. That was an age ago. Stewart's seemed the apex of luxury now. Guilt tugged at Ben. The girls were so pleased with their room but he knew it was quite a comedown from his mother's home and even the home they'd grown up in. Had he done wrong in bringing them here where there wasn't even a clapboard house?

Lizzie was tugging at him again. "This is your bedroom and Moira's. Moira won't have to sleep with us now that we're off the ship and safe. Besides, there isn't any room."

That was one more difficulty to navigate before day's end, Ben thought. The room was slightly larger than the other room, or maybe it was just that there was the one bed. What a lovely bed it was, too, with the covers already turned back, revealing clean, white linen sheets hemmed in delicately embroidered flowers that matched the hems of the pillowcases. Like in the other room, there was a washstand and trunks at the foot of the bed. Unlike the other room, this one already smelled of her. The scent of her was in the newly unpacked sheets.

"Girls, why don't you go and fetch back dinner. Take the basket and the pail and I'll have the table set when you return," Moira filled the silence with instructions and ushered them all back to the main room. The girls set off to the cook shed across the quadrangle to collect the dinner. She took down the dishes from the credenza shelves and began to lay the table. "Does the house meet with your approval?"

"My approval?" Ben chuckled and took the plates from her. "It exceeds my approval. You've worked magic here and all in one afternoon. I think the question is does it meet your approval?" He paused. "Are the girls very disappointed?"

He felt Moira's eyes on him. She set down the silverware and came to him. "Not anymore. Even a small house, when it's your own, engenders great pride."

"We will have better," he promised. "There is plenty of timber in the hills. There's talk of building a proper officer's row with real houses. It will take time, but it won't always be like this." He'd promised her decent accommodations the day he'd proposed and he had not yet kept that promise. Ben sighed. "I have to confess I'd understand if you were disappointed. The town, the fort are all of one dilapidated, underdeveloped piece. I feel as if we've landed on the backside of the world. I didn't think it would be quite like this."

What had he done in dragging this heiress into this wilderness and then expecting her to adapt to circumstances she was ill-prepared to handle? *And yet she's handled them,* his conscience prompted. *She has curtains at your window, a rug on your floor, a cloth on your table. You could not have asked for more.* But he felt he didn't deserve it.

"How could you have known?" Moira offered with a smile. "We'll do fine. This is what a blank slate looks like. Didn't you say as much to Lizzie yesterday morning?"

"Too bad the men aren't as understanding." Ben smiled back, some of the tension easing from him.

"Is it really that bad?" Moira poured cider into mugs while Ben lit the candles. It felt good to do simple domestic tasks again.

"Yes, it is, if I'm honest. We had a tour of the facility. As a fort, it's virtually useless. There are three brass guns that date back to the fifteenth century when the Spaniards first arrived and some smaller, older arms. None of them are in working order. They'll need to be drilled out and we'll need to remount them for them to be of any use. The road to town needs repair as you saw firsthand today. The kitchens are in disrepair and everything is crumbling." Despite Stevenson's claims that the men were restoring the fort, it was hard to see where progress had been made other than establishing a barracks. Of course, it had only been a few weeks and Stevenson had limited manpower.

"The men need projects and as you've said, these men aren't really meant for fighting. I think the Presidio is the perfect place for them," Moira noted with an astuteness that surprised him.

He nodded. "There will be plenty of work for wheelwrights and blacksmiths and anyone who can build. The truth of it is, I think this fort could be important if we repaired it. When I looked out over the water, I could see how close we were to it, maybe a mile. No ship can pass without us seeing it. We are in essence the guardhouse to San Francisco. The walls are thick and the view is expansive. It would be a good place to defend and to defend from if it ever came to that. It wouldn't take much manpower, either, to right the place, thank goodness."

Moira looked up from her table setting. "Why is that? I wasn't aware we were short on manpower."

"It's just that not everyone will stay on here." Ben broached the subject carefully. "Hardie's taking a company to Monterey and a company or two will sail down to Baja to join the American effort there."

Moira straightened. "Are we moving?" He could see a hundred questions cross her face and a bit of anger, too, after having put in a day of setting this house to rights.

"No, not at the moment. Company H is assigned here to the Presidio, likely for the duration." But there were no guarantees as to what that meant.

Moira smiled and said sharply, "Good," a word that carried a multitude of meanings when it came from her. There was no time to address the other issue. The girls were back with the food, a hot beef stew with bits of carrot and potato in it and a loaf of bread with butter. Ben thought it smelled divine.

It was quite possibly the best evening he'd had in a long time and hopefully a pattern for evenings to come. Good food, the good company of his family. Moira read a story out loud after supper and girls went to bed shortly afterward, both excited to try their new beds and tired from the day's activity. He and Moira sat up in the parlor, talking and sharing about their day. There was a comfortable rhythm to the conversation as they exchanged their news.

"What are your plans for tomorrow?" Ben asked.

"Weather permitting, I thought I'd take the girls to pick wildflowers and perhaps do our lessons out of doors. Yours?"

"Rebuild kitchens, reconstruct a road, drill the men, keep them from committing any kind of indecency." Ben chuckled.

"Sounds like a good time," Moira smiled across the short expanse between them, the fire light catching her hair. "I am sure the girls and I will keep ourselves busy while you rebuild the world." She meant it jokingly. But he did worry. She and the girls would be busy for a while with settling in and exploring. There would be lessons, but what would they do to occupy their time otherwise?

She would need to reconnect with the other women on the voyage and build a social network for Maggie and Lizzie. But in the next moment, Moira allayed his concerns. "I thought we might pay a call on the quartermaster's wife tomorrow, see how she and little Alta California are doing."

"That's good. I want you all to have friends here," Ben offered approvingly, aware that they'd run out of things to discuss and the night was growing late for two people who'd been up early and would have to be up early tomorrow. He was aware, too, that the issue of the bedroom could not be put off any longer.

"I'll sleep out here. I can make a pallet in front of the fire," Ben made sure there was no room for argument. This was not a question, but a statement about where he'd sleep. He thought he saw disappointment or consternation flicker briefly in Moira's gaze before it was quickly stowed away. "It's been a long day, Moira. Best get some sleep. Tomorrow will be another long day as well."

They both rose from their chairs a little stiffly, aware of a new, unresolved tension between them. "I'll get some quilts," Moira offered.

Ben nodded and stepped outside to take a short patrol to make sure all was well before he turned in. When he returned, blankets had been laid out for him by the fire, but Moira was gone, safely retired behind the bedroom door. As he readied himself for bed, the idea that he was falling in love—*again*—upended him. It was something he'd told himself he wouldn't do. To love was to open oneself to hurt. It seemed he had little choice in the latter especially when it was entirely possible he'd already fallen, perhaps weeks ago. It was too late now, a little like closing the barn door after the horse had already bolted.

Moira heard the front door close and Benjamin's footsteps on the planks as he settled for the night, out there by the fire. Away from her. It made her feel silly about her earlier worries.

A light snore came from the front room. Ben was already asleep. He was clearly satisfied with the arrangements. She should be, too. The day had been long, starting with the march from the ships and then all the unpacking and sorting. If her day had been busy, Ben's had been busy, too, perhaps busier. She'd only had two girls and three rooms to tend to. He'd had a regiment of men to oversee and a deserted fort to set in order. Yes, Ben was right. This arrangement was for the best. In the morning, when she awoke, she'd see the rightness of it even if it didn't seem that way now.

Chapter Eighteen

Spring was waking up around the Presidio. Each day the fort looked more civilized. The kitchens were repaired, pens were built for livestock and corrals for horses, barracks were cleaned for the men, parade grounds established for drill. Much as the days at sea had found their own rhythm, the days at the fort did, too.

For the men, it meant rounds of drill, construction chores and policing the hills around the fort. For Moira, it meant learning to run her little house, it meant exploring the surrounding hills in search of berries and wildflowers, and it meant lessons with the girls.

Sunny mornings were Moira's favorites. She could sit on the bench outside the house with Maggie and Lizzie and take advantage of the good weather. She alternated between them, helping Lizzie with penmanship on her slate while Maggie worked on math problems, then working with both on history. They always ended the morning with a literature lesson that involved a short lecture from her and reading out loud by the girls from whatever text or play they were studying.

It was the literature lessons that drew the most attention, subtly at first and then more overtly as the women, those who'd come over on the ships and those who'd come up from town to hire on laundresses, began to stay near the house when the girls read out loud. The women liked the plays best, with the girls reading the various parts. One shy woman, especially, tended to linger on those days, although she made a concerted effort to avoid meeting her eyes. Still, Moira noticed she came regularly and seemed to hang on every word.

"Would you like to join us?" Moira offered the following week, noting the young woman had returned yet again. "We're just beginning *As You Like It.*" Moira smiled and rose from the bench. "I'm Mrs. Sheffield and these are…my girls, Lizzie and Maggie." She couldn't keep the pride out of her voice. It was still a heady, novel experience to introduce herself that way—as a wife, as a mother. It was not something she'd ever imagined for herself in quite this way but she was feeling her way forward one day at a time.

"I'm Mrs. Mary Shelby," the woman offered quietly.

"Please, come sit," Moira invited, gesturing to the place she'd vacated on the bench. Mary Shelby glanced about, head down and nervous as if she was

afraid of being spotted. By whom? Why would anyone care if she sat for a few moments? At last the
woman sat.

"I'm pleased to meet you, Mrs. Shelby. I marvel
that we haven't met before this. You must have been
on the *Thomas Perkins*." Moira made a little small
talk, trying to place her guest. There were so few
women at the fort, it was surprising there was someone she'd not encountered yet. "We were on the *Loo
Choo*. Were you at the baptism for Alta California?"
Moira did not recall seeing her there.

"No, I was feeling poorly that day and stayed in
my cabin."

Moira smiled, sensing that her questions made
the woman uneasy. "Well, that explains it, then."
She passed Mary her copy of the play. "You haven't
missed anything, just Orlando being beaten up and
Rosalind's father being usurped. Perhaps you'd like
to read Celia's part?"

The woman looked up, meeting her gaze for the
first time, brown eyes registering shock. "Oh no,
ma'am, I couldn't. I just like to listen. I like the stories, but I can't read them myself." She flushed at the
last admission and handed the play back.

"It's no trouble. You're welcome to listen." Moira
schooled her features to hide her own shock and her
own embarrassment. She'd misstepped. She'd not
thought about the assumptions that underpinned her
invitation. This woman couldn't read, something
Moira took for granted, had taken for granted from
the age of five. The knowledge of that shook her at

her core. She nodded to Lizzie to continue, while her mind ran over what that new information meant to her. Were there others like Mary? What could she do to help them?

Mary came the next day, and the next. By Tuesday, Rosalind had disguised herself as a man to be near Orlando. By Wednesday, several romantic contretemps had taken place that threatened to expose Rosalind's true identity and Mary was joined by other women who were listening openly to the play. The quartermaster's wife sat with them, bouncing baby Alta on her knee, which encouraged others to sit as well.

Moira gave assigned parts to those who could read and encouraged everyone, reader or not, to participate in the discussions that followed the daily scene. The discussions were quite popular. Everyone had an opinion about Rosalind. Some thought her behavior scandalous, others admired her tenacity.

"She lives like a man!" one woman exclaimed in shock.

"But she also has the freedoms of a man," another woman added wistfully and debate began again. The discussions were so lively that women began bringing lunches to enjoy, transforming literature hour into an informal picnic, and the seeds of an idea began to form in Moira's mind. If they came for literary hour and the socialization that went with it, what else might they come for? Would they come to learn to read? To write? What if she could give them the tools to empower themselves to be their own Rosalinds?

Moira put the question to Ben after supper one night as they sat talking on the bench enjoying the spring evening. The girls were off to the quarter-master's to play with the baby and help his wife with chores while she and Ben had some time to themselves. These nightly conversations at the bench or walking about the fort had taken the place of their sessions at the rail of the ship. She liked the ritual and the chance it offered them to connect.

"I want to start a school," Moira told him. "What do you think of that?" His opinion mattered to her these days, far more than it had mattered that day at Stewart's when she'd obstinately bought the girls hair ribbons. They'd come along way since that day, figuratively and literally. It was an assurance she clung to, that they would conquer the distance that remained, although some days it seemed it was taking them a decidedly long time to do so.

"A school?" Ben questioned. "It's admirable, Moira, but schools need children and there are few children here at the fort. Just the girls and a couple toddlers. Perhaps in a few years, there would be enough children to support one."

"I wouldn't limit the enrollment to just fort children," Moira answered. "There are plenty of children in the area. There are some children in town. I know it's a three-mile walk but perhaps the regiment might offer a soldier or two to act as escort." After all, there was no invading army to defend against at present and it seemed to Moira that the men had time enough to escort children to and from school. "I was also thinking of inviting the Mormon children from the settlement."

The Mormons had arrived in the area in January, looking for foreign soil on which to practice their beliefs only to learn they were too late. The United States had claimed California for its own. They'd stayed anyway and settled in the hills. "It would be good for relations, Ben. Despite our differences, we all need to work together in this new place." In a new land, one couldn't have too many friends.

"It's a good idea," Ben acceded with a warm smile. "Is there anyone else you're inviting?" He was teasing her a bit but she wasn't done yet.

"Yes, matter of fact, there is." Moira dropped her voice, low and private between them. "Ben, did you know there are women here, soldiers' wives, who can't read even the most basic of sentences? I want them to come to school as well." She was thinking of Mary Shelby, who drank up every word of *As You Like It* and yet couldn't access such enjoyment for herself.

"Moira, not every woman here is you. They haven't had your advantages," Ben began and she couldn't quite read his reaction.

"Of course not, but now they can," Moira pressed cautiously. She'd learned Ben respected honest discussion, but he did not appreciate outright defiant argument. "Can you imagine not being able to read a newspaper or a letter from home? To have to rely on others for your information? To not be able to read your Bible? How can a woman be responsible for educating her children if she's not educated herself?" Her education was something Ben had said he'd appreciated about her. Before he'd even really known her, he'd seen the value of having an educated woman in his household for his daughters.

Ben nodded slowly. "Where do you plan on putting this school, Moira?"

Moira flashed him a wide smile. "Here, right outside the house. I was hoping you could put up a canvas awning as protection against the days it rains."

"I'll do it tomorrow," Ben promised but there was a sigh in his voice.

"Does the school not please you?" Moira searched his face for reasons behind his reticence, worry forming in her stomach. She'd expected more joyful support from him. Why would he not want to extend the gift of learning that he wanted for his daughters to other women as well? She'd not taken him for a hypocrite.

"Have I misjudged you?" she challenged even as her heart sank. After all these months, did she still not know her husband? Just when she thought she knew him, there was always another layer to pull back. What would she do if the man for whom she'd developed a warm, caring regard was not all she thought him to be?

"Of course not, Moira," he assured her with a certain solemnity. "It's a marvelous idea. I've agreed to hang the awning, haven't I?"

"Then what is it?" She'd thought he'd be pleased she'd found a way to channel her efforts into the community they were building here at the fort.

His hand reached for hers. "I don't want you to be disappointed. Not everyone will agree with you. Some women simply won't see the need for it, or have the time for it. Some men, too."

"No one is forcing them to come, it's just on offer." Would Mary Shelby with her furtive gazes and nerves take the offer?

"It's generous of you Moira." Ben ran his thumb over her knuckles. "Remember, it's one thing to be a teacher. It's another to be a crusader. Do you think I don't listen to the literary discussions your group holds? I hear them and the men hear them, too." He gave a friendly chuckle but his words were serious. "You're not just teaching them to read, you're teaching them to think. Some men will be intimidated by that. Just be careful, that's all."

Moira nodded her promise. She was getting used to being careful: careful when she took the girls out to pick flowers, careful with her husband when he slept on his pallet before the fire. Being careful was new to her. She could no longer rush headlong into things. People were counting on her now, people she cared about.

Ben squeezed her hand and rose, getting ready to make his nightly patrol of the stockade. "Moira, thank you for asking. I appreciate that you came to me, that you wanted to consult me." He brought her hand to his lips and kissed it with a smile. "You're an admirable woman. The girls and I are fortunate to have you here with us and we know it."

It was a generous compliment, and yet as he walked away to make his nightly rounds, Moira couldn't help but wish the pronouns in that compliment had been different, that he hadn't needed to couple himself with the girls. What she wouldn't give to hear him say *he* was fortunate to have her here with *him*. It was a sign that they'd come far but they still had a ways to go, at least for her. She didn't want their matrimonial journey to end there. Did he?

Be patient, she reminded herself, never mind that she was no more skilled at patience than she was caution, but she was learning. For all things there was a season.

Chapter Nineteen

The lessons became a gateway to cultivating relationships with the other women over the weeks that followed, not just at the fort, but in the area. In that way, the school she'd created was fulfilling one of its purposes at least. In others, Ben's predictions had proved true. Even women who wanted to learn were less than reliable students. They came when they could, citing chores and obligations at home that prevented regular attendance.

In many cases, Moira thought the obstacles weren't so much chores as husbands. Most worrisome was Mary Shelby, who had made remarkable early progress, then she'd come to class with a bruised cheek and a few days later stopped coming altogether. When Moira spoke of it to Ben, however, he cautioned her not to meddle in another man's marriage. But he did promise to see what he could do. "Pick your battles, Moira," he counseled, as they sat outside on a spring evening in April, enjoying the air. "You won't win them all and you just had a victory in getting the Mormon children here. Celebrate what you can. The school is doing well."

And it was. "The Fort School," as it was called now, had swelled to a population of twenty-five. The quartermaster's wife was now helping her manage them all and she'd even given Maggie some responsibilities with the younger children to hone Maggie's own skills. "It's good advice, given that I have plans to expand." She slid her gaze sideways to catch Ben's reaction.

"Expand? Will there be any room under your awning?" Ben teased, but there was a glimmer of pride in his eyes. He was proud of her little school and her efforts at the fort despite his counsel to caution.

Moira felt it made up for the things she wasn't good at: laundry, and cooking, both of which she still relied heavily on others for help. She took much of their laundry to the laundresses who cared for the men's uniforms, and she picked up dinner from the mess kitchens, unable to manage more than boiling water and toasting bread in the fireplace.

"Now who are you thinking of inviting?" Ben inquired.

"The native children and the Spaniards," Moira began carefully, aware that those groups might be even more controversial, given the politics of the war, than the subject of educating women. "We can gather for an-exchange-of-language lessons, each one helping the other. The children can all learn Spanish and English and the native tongues." She thought that would appeal to Ben and his love of languages. Of all the people here, Ben would understand their importance as a means of building relationships between people and cultures.

Ben nodded thoughtfully. "It's a noble goal, Moira." Somewhere in the distance crickets chirped and an owl hooted. Moira waited for Ben to say the rest. "I don't know you'll get permission for it, though, from the commander, and you will need it." He was deadly serious.

"Whyever not?" Moira turned to face him on the bench. "It's a great opportunity for the children to interact with other children, to learn new languages, and to build for the future. California is all these people living together."

"The military sees them as defeated peoples, Moira. Inviting them into the fort is a potential security risk. It exposes us, or so I am told." She heard the distaste for the argument in his voice. "I don't like it any more than you do."

"Defeated peoples? I despise that term," Moira scoffed. "How is there ever to be real peace if people keep insisting on defining everyone as winners and losers? It's ridiculous."

Ben shook his head. Tonight there was a tension in him that came from somewhere deep down. Something was on his mind, perhaps the same something that had been on his mind since the first day they'd arrived. But she'd learned Ben could not be rushed. He would talk when he was ready.

"I despise the terms, the conditions, too." Ben sighed. "This is beautiful land—the water, the trees, the hills. The soil is rich, and even the scent in the air is unique to this place. But beautiful things aren't being done here. Every day that passes, it becomes more clear and I cannot continue, in good conscience, to ignore it, to pretend that I am not contributing to it."

"What do you think you're contributing to?" Moira asked quietly, unable to fathom what corruption her good, strong husband was participating in . She saw him working with the men every day, shirt-sleeves rolled up as they raised buildings and repaired old ones. She saw him in his uniform, drilling his men on the parade grounds, and her heart swelled with pride in knowing how hard he worked, and with the selfish pride that this man was hers. The women would comment about him on occasion, remarking about how handsome he was, how strong and how considerate.

"We are an army of occupation. I knew that when I signed on. I didn't think it would be like this, though. They hate us. When we ride out on patrol, I see the distrust and the dislike in their faces. I feel shame over what we've done. We've taken this land for no other reason than to simply have more of it. Who are we to tell people how to worship or live or what language to speak? I want peace but not like this. This isn't real peace, it's enforced peace." Ben let out a breath and she could feel the despair in him. "I wanted a fresh start. I thought I would walk off the ship into an empty, pristine land. But now I see that my fresh start comes at a very significant price paid by others."

His sense of justice could not countenance such a price. Moira reached for his hand. "What do you suggest we do?" Although she feared the answer. "Do you think we should leave?" She didn't want to go. It wasn't just the daunting prospect of another six-month journey by ship so soon. It was that she didn't *want* to abandon her fledgling school, her little house. She was making a place here with him. She wasn't ready to give that up.

Ben shook his head. "Leaving solves nothing. Now that I've seen the situation firsthand, I can't unsee it. Leaving means I'd only be ignoring it from a distance, and that's a whole other level of hypocrisy." He put his other hand over Moira's, his voice dropping. "I've been thinking of resigning."

The announcement stunned her. "But you love the military."

"But I'd always planned to leave at some point and establish the grocery." He gave her a wry smile. "Or maybe you and I should establish a school, since you've proven so apt at it."

"Do you think San Francisco could support a greengrocery?" Moira furrowed her brow. There were only a handful of people there. She couldn't imagine them making a living.

"The military is coming. Kearney's troops are here from overland. You saw all those ships in the harbor when we arrived. This is just the beginning.

Might as well get in on the ground floor. It will take time to establish relationships with the farmers. They'll be our supply chain. But we can sell their produce in town near the ships, and we can get contracts with the military for fresh fruits and vegetables." His smile widened. "I can build you a good house in town, Moira, one that is worthy of your silver candlesticks and china."

"*This* house is worthy of them," she insisted. "Will you think on it? Pray on it, Ben? Perhaps the regiment will be mustered out soon and the point of resigning will be moot."

"That's good counsel, thank you for it, Moira." Ben smiled and rose, stretching, ready to make his patrol, and she felt a thrill of wifely pride in knowing that he'd come to her with something on his heart and had appreciated her advice as she had done with him concerning the school earlier. It was further proof that there was hope for more between them. He was starting to look upon her as a helpmate.

"There's one more thing." Ben's eyes twinkled. "I need to send my dress uniform to the laundry. I need to look my best for the officers' ball."

"Ball?" A little trill of excitement went through her at the prospect of some entertainment, but more so at the thought of dancing with Ben.

"We'll have a little orchestra and hold it on the parade grounds. It was just announced today." Ben gave her a wide grin. "You can wear one of your fancy New York dresses. If you could have Senorita Consuela have my uniform ready, I could perhaps match you in brilliance," Ben laughed. "She does a wonderful job, gets the starch at the collar just right."

"I'll take it tomorrow," Moira promised with a smile she didn't feel. Consuela had come to the fort looking for work after the men had arrived. She was young and pretty and she lavished all kinds of attention on the men, especially the officers with money. She'd shown particular deference to Ben over the weeks, doing his laundry first and doing it spectacularly. Everything was well pressed and fresh smelling when Moira picked it up. But it was clear young Consuela thought her an inadequate wife in not doing her husband's laundry.

Moira stood in line the next morning with others dropping off laundry, trying to ignore that most of the others in line were single men. When she reached the front of the line, Consuela gave her that smug smile she'd come to dread.

"For the ball?" Consuela surmised. "I'll have it ready. Major Sheffield is a very handsome man." She made a little moue of concern as she leaned forward. "Is the major well, senora? I thought he looked a bit thin the other day. I thought to myself, there's a man who needs some tamales." She reached behind her and handed Moira a package wrapped in dried corn sheaves. "I made them myself, for Major Sheffield. We can't have him sicken. There are not so many good men in the world. It's a shame when one goes wanting for lack of a good meal."

Moira's temper flared. "My husband is very well,

thank you." But she didn't dare give the tamales back, it would officially signal war between them and publicly, too. It would call attention to Ben and to herself. She remembered too clearly the business with Thomas Elliott and the speculation that had run about the ship early on in the voyage regarding their marriage. Such repeat speculation would hatch those rumors anew. "Thank you for thinking us, though, with the tamales. We are eager to try all the new foods."

She turned and stalked away before her patience failed her. How dare that woman imply she wasn't taking care of her husband, and out loud where she could be overheard. It was one thing with that smirk—someone might interpret that smile in multiple ways—but words were another. The woman had issued a challenge. One that Moira couldn't rightly argue with. She was trembling with rage at the laundress and disappointment in herself.

Was she taking care of Ben as a wife should? She was doing her best. She knew Ben was proud of her school and proud of how their little house looked. She could dust and sweep and wash dishes. She kept his decanter filled with cider and flowers on the table. She kept the bed made, the sheets changed. But she didn't wash his sheets, she didn't wash his clothes, or press them. She could no more get the starch in his collar right than the man on the moon.

"Mama Moira, are you alright?" Lizzie looked up from her slate where she was practicing her handwriting before lessons started.

"I'm fine." She expelled a breath and made a decision. Under no circumstance was she serving those tamales for dinner. *She* would cook dinner for her husband tonight. She'd mastered tea and toast in the fireplace; certainly she could manage biscuits and stew. "I was just thinking that I might end lessons a bit early today so I can make dinner. It's time we start cooking more at home and relying on the mess tent a little less."

Dinner wasn't so hard, after all. Moira was feeling quite pleased with herself as she tossed the last of the carrots into the pot hanging on the hob over the fire. She'd managed to chop carrots, slice potatoes and dice up chunks of rabbit meat and throw it all into the boiling pot. She'd also managed biscuits to slide in on a rack a little latter. She wiped her hands on her apron and set about fixing the table. She'd fed the tamales to Maggie and Lizzie earlier and sent them to watch baby Alta for the evening, giving the quartermaster and his wife a much-needed break.

Dinner for two. Moira stepped back to survey the table, pleased. Perhaps a quiet homemade dinner without the girls would be just the right setting in which to bring up the other topic on her mind— the status of their marriage.

Ben arrived home, prompt as usual. "What is this? Where are Maggie and Lizzie?"

"Dinner, for us. The girls are at the quartermaster's helping out." Moira felt a familiar trill of excitement go through her. "I cooked it myself. Stew and biscuits." She was excited for him to taste it. She would prove to him she could be a good wife, not just a mother to his daughters but a helpmate to him as well.

She was so proud. Ben could feel the sense of pride and accomplishment rolling off her. She'd taken care with the table, and a little extra care with her appearance, although Moira always looked nice. Tonight, she'd put on a bit of perfume, just enough to tempt a man to lean in closer for a better whiff. Ben sat at the table and asked the blessing. He dipped his spoon into his bowl for that first taste, determined not to disappoint her. How bad could it be after all? He'd eaten plenty of poor food at Fort Brady.

The admonition didn't help. It couldn't make the potatoes less hard, the carrots less crunchy, and it couldn't make the meat more tender, but it was hot and that was a start. Perhaps if he took smaller bites? Ben reached for a biscuit. He knew from experience that bread could work wonders and there was promise here; the biscuit seemed firm on the outside. He dipped the biscuit into the broth and took a bite only to be met with gooey, sticky dough inside. The biscuit was uncooked. There would be no help for him there.

Across the table, Moira watched him expectantly. "How is it?"

Ben swallowed. "Fine. It's just fine." God would understand the necessity for the lie.

She smiled and for a moment that smile made up

for the bites he'd have to choke down to get through
the meal. She dipped her own spoon and ate, the expression on her face changing from satisfied to horrified. She spit a potato back into her bowl. "This is
awful!" she said with her customary boldness.

"No, it's not," Ben insisted, spooning up another
mouthful. "You must have just gotten a bad piece
of meat."

"No, I didn't. The stew's all bad." Moira reached
for a biscuit and ripped it open, her face crumbling at
the sight of the doughy insides. "The biscuits aren't
even cooked through." She threw the biscuit on the
table in disgust. For the food? For herself? For both?

"It's fine, Moira. We have bread left from this
morning, and there's cheese. Why don't I just toast
us a few slices." Ben was already up and moving.
"One meal isn't the end of the world." But he'd misjudged the import of this one. Moira burst into tears,
the very last thing he'd come to expect from her.

"It's not just the meal," she sobbed. "I can't cook.
I can't even make biscuits. I am not taking care of
you, Ben. What sort of wife can't even make biscuits? And everyone knows it! Consuela gave me
tamales today when I took your uniform over. She
said you were looking thin. I'm a failure, Ben. I run
a school, but it's not even a real school, it's for who-
ever shows up on whatever day, but it's all I can do."

Ben set aside the bread. "You're not a failure,
Moira. You do a lot of things. You're great with the
girls, with the school, with making this little house a
home. You will learn to cook, but even if you don't,

it doesn't matter. We can live on mess hall dinners, we can hire a cook when I'm out of the army." That topic again. Why did she feel as if that was somehow her fault, too?

She raised her head, her face tear stained. "I'm supposed to be your wife. A wife is supposed to do things and everyone knows I don't. Consuela…"

"Will no longer be doing my laundry," Ben said grimly. "If she has caused you anguish, I will have words with her." There, that should put an end to Moira's tears. All he wanted was for her to stop crying. Moira was strong, tenacious. "Besides, since when do you care what anyone thinks, Moira?"

"When that person is you, Ben."

Chapter Twenty

The words nearly dropped him. Moira *cared* for him. The realization swept over him in a wave of powerful emotion. "I thought this was about Consuela and her insults." He wasn't sure where this conversation was heading. How had a ruined dinner become about him?

"You can't fault Consuela for telling the truth, that I'm not caring for you as a wife should. Perhaps if you'd only waited to wed, you could have had a woman here better suited to the environment."

"I don't want a woman suited to the environment, Moira. I want a woman who is suited to *me*, and that woman is you," Ben said in all seriousness. It was unnerving to see her like this. She'd survived so much since leaving New York that it seemed all the more devastating that raw stew and biscuits could undo her. He didn't want her to break.

"I want to be your wife, Ben."

"Are you not?" Ben argued. "Did I not share with you my political concerns about being here? Did you not come to me with your concerns for a school? Do we not talk every night about the girls and our lives here? Have I not shared with you my hopes for life after the military? Surely, that is how a husband treats a wife whom he trusts with his thoughts, with his mind, with the raising of his children."

Not want her? Is that what she thought? Did she not realize he went to sleep thanking the Lord for having sent her to him, that every time he saw her with his daughters his heart soared at the joy she'd brought back to them? He went to her and gathered her close, his heart bursting and breaking all at once, and yet he could not find the words to say all that was within him when it came to her. To tell her that he'd fallen for her time and again from the day in Rio to the night she'd prayed with him over Lizzie and every day since. That he could not believe his good fortune that such a woman might care for a difficult, closed off man like himself. He hoped his touch might say what he could not put into words.

Had she not already guessed how he felt, what he felt? If so, that was his fault. A wife should not be in doubt of her worth. *A good woman is worth more than rubies.* Moira had proved to be that and more. Still, he was not a naive man.

They were two people who'd only known each other for eight months and under unique circumstances. It was never far from his mind that under more normal circumstances, Moira would not have chosen him, would not even have noticed him. Indeed, she'd not noticed him at all at the house party. But they were noticing each other now, forced to it or not, and in that notice there was a growing attraction based not just on proximity but something more—mutual respect and hope. Hope that each could change; hope that he could find his way to love again, and hope that she could curb untamed tendencies to act before thinking. That hope was a work in progress and Ben was content to wait. He needed Moira to understand that.

He swept away her tears with his hand. He saw the pulse at the base of her neck give a little leap of satisfaction. He felt it, too. *When* was a word of promise, a word of future hope. Soon, it would be time to make her his wife in truth.

A party at the Presidio was long overdue and the fort was abustle with the excitement. That excitement mirrored Moira's own. A sense of exhilaration had run just beneath the surface of her skin all week and went straight to the bone. Her exhilaration had to do with more than the impending ball. She and Ben would be husband and wife in truth soon. It was as if the journey was truly nearing completion, that this was what she'd been meant to find: a fulfillment with another person that made her whole. This was where she was meant to be—with Ben, wherever he went, whatever he did.

"Moira, are you ready?" Ben peered into the bedroom, already resplendent in his dress uniform. He'd dressed in the parlor while the girls had piled into the bedroom to assist with her hair. Now, Maggie and Lizzie were off again to watch baby Alta for the evening.

"Almost, I just need help with my necklace." Moira held up a strand of pearls. He took them from her, his hands warm against her skin. She'd chosen a vibrant, deep blue gown that exposed her shoulders and cinched in her waist with its tight bodice. She'd packed it and a few other dresses highly unsuitable for San Francisco in a moment of whimsy and perhaps hope that she'd have a chance to wear something so fine again. Tonight, she was glad for it. Especially when Ben was looking at her with pride. She wanted him to be proud of her, wanted him to enjoy spending the evening with her. It was going to be a beautiful night with everyone all dressed up and dancing beneath the stars.

"You look quite fine, Mrs. Sheffield," He reached for her hand and kissed it. "Shall we go?"

It was a short walk on a warm spring evening to the parade grounds where the ball was held. The space had been transformed with a temporarily laid planked dance floor and a raised dais for the little six-piece orchestra cobbled together from the men. Benches and trestle tables were set out for resting and refreshment. The tables boasted an enormous silver punch bowl, courtesy of Colonel Stevenson, and trays of breads and cakes. Lanterns had been hung for light as the sun set over the bay beyond.

"It looks beautiful." Moira sighed wistfully at the

sight. "No New York ballroom could look better. I hadn't realized how much I'd missed a chance to go out until now." She twirled on Ben's arm. "Tonight, I want to dance until there are holes in my slippers."

"I'm sure that can be managed," Ben chuckled. With the shortage of women, everyone would be pressed into service to make sure all the men would have the chance to dance. A few carriages, wagons and horses had come up from town on the newly improved road for the festivities. Vallejo and Prudhorn had been invited as well to celebrate the reestablishment of the fort.

The men were well-turned out in their uniforms. The laundresses must have been busy, Moira thought, surveying the crowd. The women, too, were dressed in their Sunday best and the stage was set for a gay evening. The orchestra tuned up and the dancing began. Ben whirled her through a reel and another country dance before generously relinquishing her to Cort Visser, the first of many partners.

The evening was a blur of smiles. Ben partnered with her again later on, stealing her for a polka, his hand firm at her waist. "I think you're the evening's favorite," he laughed. "Every man here is smitten with you and I can see why." He leaned close. "You're by the far the prettiest one."

"You might be biased." She flashed him a playful smile as they cut across the dance floor.

"You look happy," Ben said. "Are you?"

"So happy, Ben. I did not believe such happiness was possible." She'd been chasing happiness for years, she realized now, using her pranks and outrageous behavior to fill a void that could never be filled with such risks. Happiness was a different thrill altogether.

Ben swung her in a tight turn and she tipped her head back to the sky, laughing up at the stars, happiness spilling from her. Mrs. Bostwick would chastise her for being so ridiculous but Mrs. Bostwick was thousands of miles away. Here, she was happy, dancing in the arms of the man she loved. Nothing could take that joy away.

Ben relinquished her once again under the pretense of needing to speak with Major Visser. She found herself in the arms of Captain Shelby, Mary's husband. Mary had not been back to lessons for quite some time and Moira had only seen the woman at a distance. She missed Mary and she thought perhaps Mary missed the school as well. The young woman had made rapid progress and had shown a real aptitude for learning. It seemed unlikely to Moira that Mary would have chosen to stop coming of her own volition.

In her exuberance over the evening, Moira thought maybe she could use this dance to help Mary's cause. Perhaps in Shelby's own high spirits he might be persuaded to encourage his wife to attend again.

"Are you enjoying the evening, Captain?" Moira smiled up at him, taking his measure. He was a tall, lean man with a whipcord strength to him. Despite her smile, he didn't seem the least bit taken with her. He only grunted in response. She tried again. "I'm sure Mary is enjoying an evening out. She works hard. Has she recovered from her bruise?"

His dark eyes narrowed and his grip on her tightened. "What do you know about that bruise? What did she say?"

"Nothing, only that she fell." Not that Moira had believed that. Most people didn't bruise their faces when they fell. She believed it even less now that she was dancing with Mary's unfriendly husband.

"That's right. She fell. That's all. She fell because she was clumsy and she was hurrying. She wouldn't have been rushing if she'd not been at your school instead of at home where she belongs." He glared at her. She'd not encountered such unveiled aggression from a man before. It was positively frightening even here on a dance floor surrounded by people and her husband here in the crowd somewhere. "If you're wondering why I wanted to dance with you, Mrs. Sheffield, it's to remind you of your place. Women don't need education and they don't need it from the likes of you."

"Husbands should educate their wives, then," Moira shot back, some of the happiness of the evening slipping away. She felt fire rumble deep within, the desire to fight, to resist.

"What for? Don't need an education to have a baby or cook a meal. You're proof enough of that, ain't you?" He leered. "You can't cook a meal to save your life, I hear, and you ain't in the family way. Don't know what Major Sheffield sees in you. You look like a right lost cause to me, a fancy woman out of her depth. Ain't no call for it out here." His gaze mocked her.

"This dance is over, Captain Shelby. If you'll excuse me." Moira made to pull away but Shelby held her fast.

"The dance is over when I say it's over. I'm not done with you yet. You need to know there are a lot of men who don't hold with you educating the women. They have chores to do and you are taking them away from their duties. You are filling their heads with nonsense about what they can be, what they can want. They can't be anything but wives, Mrs. Sheffield. You will only disappoint them and wreck their marriages in the long run. What you need is a good strapping, some sense beaten right into you."

The man was positively odious. She wanted to be away from him. She tried again to wrest free but he held firm. Did Ben see them? Did he see she was not enjoying the dance? "Take your hands off me, right now," she ordered but he only laughed, cruel and harsh.

"Now, there's talk of you wanting to bring native kids in and the like. Pretty soon you'll have us all speaking Spanish if your husband doesn't man up and do his duty to keep his woman in line. If he doesn't, I've a mind to do it myself. You, ma'am, have become a security risk."

Moira was furious. "I have *never* been talked to in such a manner."

"Perhaps that's why you're so uppity. A thrash-

ing would do you good." He held her so close now
she could smell the distinct scent of alcohol on his
breath. The man was not only rude but drunk.

"Perhaps a thrashing might help *you* learn some
manners," A gruff voice came from behind Shelby.
"Take your hands off my wife."

Ben! Relief swept Moira as Shelby turned away
from her. But relief was short-lived. Shelby was
spoiling for a fight and determined to have one.

"Seems as if you need a little help managing your
wife, Sheffield," Shelby growled.

"Not from the likes of you." Ben's eyes glittered
dangerously. "You're drunk. Go home, sleep it off.
You're done dancing tonight." Ben gestured for two
men to help Shelby from the dance floor but Shelby
shook them off.

"I'm done when I say I'm done." Something
flashed in Shelby's fist and Moira gasped. A knife!
She watched in horror as Shelby moved first, slash-
ing at Ben with the blade. Ben was ready for him,
catching the man around the waist and coming up
underneath the knife. His hand shackled the man's
wrist and the two went down, punching and kicking
in a struggle for the knife. A circle formed around
them as people gathered to watch. The ball had officially become a brawl.

The fight didn't last long. Ben didn't spare her a
glance until Shelby was subdued and led off by Cort
Visser to the fort jail. The crowd dispersed and returned to dancing but whispers were already starting,
whispers about her, and about the fight. Officers did

not conduct themselves that way, not without penalty. Ben would pay for this outburst—*her* outburst.

Moira was shaking by the time Ben wrapped his coat about her. "I'm sorry, it's all my fault. I shouldn't have struggled. I should have let him spew his vile words. They were just words."

"They were not just words. He threatened you." Ben led her into the shadows beyond the dance floor where they might have some privacy. "Are you alright?" He was still vibrating with the energy of the fight. She could feel it rolling off him.

"I'm fine. I should be asking you the same. You were the one he tried to stab." Her voice trembled over the last and she fell against him. The knife had been too real. One slice and she could have lost him. His arm was about her, his voice murmuring assurances at her ear.

"I'm unhurt, Moira. I'm harder to kill than that." He rocked her, soothing her, but her mind was racing.

"Will you be punished?" Horrid images of a flogging filled her mind. She couldn't stand it if he were hurt for her, debased for her. Again came the thought this was her fault. Ben had warned her about the school, about meddling in another's marriage. She'd not listened.

"I doubt it. He started it and he had a weapon. I had no choice but to act in self-defense." Ben dismissed the concern. "Let me take you home."

It was the right decision but Moira's heart mourned the fact that the evening was over. Even in the comfort of their home, the happiness had gone from the evening. What she'd done tonight was Edward Brant and Thomas Elliott all over again, only this had been so much worse than any of those incidents. This had involved a weapon, and someone other than herself had paid for her actions. When would she learn?

Never. The answer made her miserable as she lay in bed, the lamp blown out. She'd not thought the night would end like this, alone in the dark, her happiness stripped from her, exposed for the fragile thing it was. She ruined everything she touched even when she meant well. Her mind threw recriminations in a relentless barrage. *Deep down you know you don't deserve happiness. You're not good enough, not like your brother or Ben. Now you've made things difficult for Ben when he's been nothing but good to you. He'll want you to leave...*

It would not be her choice this time as it had been in Rio. He would demand it now. He and the girls were settled. They didn't need her. She'd brought them nothing but trouble. She wasn't capable of anything else. It was a harsh realization to fall asleep on.

Chapter Twenty-One

The summons came the next morning as they were finishing breakfast, delivered by two aides from the colonel's office. Major Sheffield was to report to Colonel Stevenson immediately. The men would wait until the major was ready to leave. Moira exchanged a glance with Ben across the table, worried. It was a reminder that leaving him couldn't spare him from what had already happened, only from what might happen in the future.

"It's nothing, Moira. The colonel speaks with me often. It's likely about the report from last week," he assured her with a final swallow of coffee.

Moira wasn't convinced. The colonel didn't usually leave men behind to make sure a summons was answered. She still wasn't convinced an hour later when she went out to gather her ration of eggs from the mess kitchen coops. She told herself no news was good news but in this case it was like waiting for the storm to break. There was something in the air, the fort fairly vibrated with it. There was a bristling sense of urgency in the way the men walked and talked. There was more activity, too, especially by the horse corrals.

Slowly, rumors began to circulate. A party was riding out from the fort. A nugget of worry formed in her stomach. Something she told herself was entirely irrational. Patrols rode out all the time. There was regular trouble with gangs of horse thieves. But this *felt* different. Still, it didn't mean Ben was taking the patrol out. He wasn't even scheduled to ride out, having done a patrol last week. She went home and waited. Surely, if something was wrong Ben would have come and told her. But nothing she told herself, no matter how reasonable, could still the foreboding.

Would he come to tell her? The thought taunted her. The people they'd been before last night would have. Those two had begun to open themselves to one another. But last night, she'd caused trouble, forcing him to defend her with his fists, possibly at the expense of his career. She'd put him in an untenable situation and dragged him down with her. He owed her nothing. Despite his parting reassurances, he'd been quiet over breakfast and they'd not had time to say anything to one another. She'd had no time to apologize, to tell him she would be on the first ship to New York. She could at least spare him having to ask her to leave. She could do that much for him, take the blame so that he would not have to carry that burden, too.

Ben came home at eleven, looking grim. Before he even spoke, she knew her worry hadn't been misplaced. She rose and went to him, a gesture born of habit. "What's happened?"

Ben brushed past her, opening the trunk where he kept his clothes, his tone as brisk as his step. "I'm home only for a moment. I'm needed to ride out with some men to take care of a problem. A band of rustlers has been causing trouble. We're going to clean out their den. Orders from Monterey," That was where the military governor was stationed.

Moira tried to take the news calmly. It wasn't as if the whole regiment had been shipped down to Baja or off to some of the fighting still going on farther south. "I thought the men here were to be used for police action only." She willed her mind to think through it critically. What did this have to do with last night?

"Cleaning out rustlers *is* policing work. No one's horses or livestock are secure with rustlers on the loose and in these parts where we are isolated from any support, a horse is one of a man's most valuable commodities," Ben reminded her. Horses were indeed a precious luxury. The other luxury was a man's gun.

"I know, it just seems more dangerous." When Ben went out on patrol it usually involved riding through the hills and checking in with the American settlers, riding out to the ranches and Indian camps. There was tension certainly, but no trouble. But there was more behind this, if only she could sort it out.

Ben finished stuffing a clean shirt into a saddle-bag. "It will just be a couple of days at the most. We'll camp tonight, take care of them tomorrow and be home by evening if we ride hard, or early the next day." Those three days would be the longest of her life, Moira thought. Three days until Ben was home safe with her again.

Moira knitted her brow. That didn't seem right. "You just went out on patrol. Another group should go."

Ben's reply was brisk. "The patrol is Shelby's. He's in no shape to lead such a mission at the moment. He's hungover and has to answer for his behavior last night." He paused and she felt his eyes rest on her. "Moira, leadership is a privilege. Letting Shelby command a mission would send the wrong message about leadership and behavior to the men." But there was another message for another man, too. Ben. Taking Shelby's place was Ben's consequence for fighting, for taking matters into his own hands. On her behalf. This was her fault, came the reminder that had incessantly flogged her.

"It makes no sense to send you into danger while he gets to stay safely behind. He's the one who accosted me and he's the one being rewarded by staying here." Moira's temper blazed, fueled by guilt and upset.

"This is how it is in the army. There are orders and they must be followed," Ben said curtly. His curtness was her fault, too. He was angry with her because of it. He knew what had happened and why even if he was being careful not to say so. He was being careful to ignore her, too. He was all brisk action; he had no time for her. She was being dismissed like he'd dismissed her during the early days on the ship.

Moira stepped in front of him. "Ben, please, wait. Surely, we have a moment. We have to talk about last night. It's the reason this is happening. This is my fault. If Stevenson wants to punish someone, it should be me. Let me go to him, let me explain."

Ben's gaze was hard blue stone. "Absolutely not. You do that, and it proves Shelby was right, that I can't control my own wife." He shook his head. "You've always been wild, Moira. You've been used to there being a way to fix things after you've charged through, but not this time. I have to do this." Grim anger radiated from him and she hated it, hated being the reason for it. She'd gone too far and she would lose him over this. He could not forgive her, and he could not redeem her as her brother had hoped marriage to him would.

"I don't want you to leave in anger." Moira was close to begging.

Ben interrupted, stern and brusque. "Moira, I *cannot* discuss this right now. I have to go. I've asked the quartermaster to keep an eye out for you. I don't think there will be any difficulty with Shelby." He reached into his trunk a final time. "However, I seem to recall you're a pretty good shot." He passed her the pistol. "If Shelby troubles you and the girls, shoot him. But Moira, don't kill him." Ben picked up his saddlebags. "I'll stop at the quartermaster's to say goodbye to Maggie and Lizzie."

Moira swallowed against the tightness in her throat. This would be the last time she saw him, if she could manage it and find a ship sailing before he returned. He would not need to worry about her again. She would leave the moment she knew he was home safe. But oh, how it hurt to think of leaving the girls and leaving him. She was not worthy of them. She struggled not to cry. What sort of officer's wife went to pieces when her husband went out on a simple mission? If she couldn't cook biscuits, she could at least be brave. Ben deserved that much at least from her.

"Be safe, Ben," she said, knowing he would not welcome anything more in farewell, another sign of how much she'd wrecked between them. Then he was gone.

The girls came running home shortly after that. She hugged them to her, offering them reassurance that this was nothing more than a simple clearing of outlaws.

The call to assemble went up and Moira took the girls outside to watch the soldiers pass. The whole fort, it seemed, had turned out to send the group off. Ten men, with Ben and Cort at the head of the column, rode off smartly on their horses to the cheers of their fellow soldiers. For many of the men in the group, it was their first real action. Ben and Cort had experience, of course, but these other men did not.

That realization worried Moira greatly. These

were not seasoned veterans or West Point cadets. These were volunteers who'd come here looking for a new life after their service was done. She chided herself for her doubts. Ben and Cort had drilled them, they were better prepared than when they'd set sail. Besides, outlaw rustlers weren't trained soldiers, either. It wasn't as if they were riding out to meet an invading army, she reminded herself. But no reminder could override the nagging guilt that ate at her: if anything happened to Ben on the mission, it would be her fault. He wouldn't be riding out if not for her and the trouble she'd caused.

Once the excitement of the muster and departure had passed, Moira held school beneath the awning as if it were an ordinary day, ignoring the fact that many women hadn't come today. She helped the children with their lessons, which made the afternoon pass quickly. But she was keenly aware of being alone. The men in Ben's company weren't married men. They'd not left wives behind to commiserate with. The other women at the fort were either unattached, or they were the wives of other officers—officers who'd not been required to go out.

Moira and the girls retired to bed early that evening, exhausted by the day's events. She'd kept up a good front through dinner, entertaining Maggie and Lizzie with a story afterward. But now, with the girls abed for the night, she had to face her guilt. If she'd not irritated Shelby at the ball last night, Ben would be home safe. Shelby would be the one riding out, hungover or not. Had it only been last night she'd been dancing beneath the stars in Ben's arm thinking her happiness was complete and unassailable, that it could not be shaken?

Perhaps it could not be shaken, Moira thought, tossing restlessly. But it could be taken and it had been. *Please, Lord, keep him safe. I love him so.* Even if she had to leave him to keep him safe. Did she dare pray? Would God answer? She hadn't Ben's unadulterated faith. Hers was a faith broken in childhood and glued back together in a mishmash of belief and doubt; belief that God was real but doubt that He watched over her, that He would answer if she called upon him. With arguments like that, one thing was certain: it was definitely going to be a long night.

And a long day. Exhausted from lack of sleep and emotional worry, Moira found herself looking incessantly toward the gates of the fort as evening neared. But no men came. It was no cause for alarm, she repeated to herself as she set out dinner for the girls—rabbit stew from the mess kitchen and some of Cook's flaky biscuits. She poured mugs of cider and felt tears sting the backs of her eyes. Cider would forever be associated with Ben. She sat with the girls and picked at her food but she was edgy, wanting to be back outside where she could see the gate even though night was falling and it was unlikely the men would be traveling in the dark over unfamiliar terrain. Just as it was unlikely the men would return tonight in any event.

There was a knock at the door shortly after eight, very late for a social call. Moira's heart thumped.

Was it bad news? Was it Shelby? She opened the door just a crack to see the quartermaster's wife standing there, baby and basket in hand. "I've come to see how you're doing." The woman offered her a friendly smile as Moira opened the door more fully. She swept inside. "Seems I've come just in time. Looks like you haven't slept a wink. I hardly sleep myself with all the getting up with the baby and such. So, I thought to myself, why not go and see how Moira and the girls are getting on." She handed Moira the baby and the basket to Maggie. "I baked tarts this afternoon if you're in the mood for a treat."

The woman sat down and took out her mending as another knock sounded announcing a new arrival. "You and the girls will have company tonight. Shouldn't have let you three be alone last night," she said with a smile.

By the time the knocks at the door fell silent, four of the fort's women had arrived to gather about Moira in the front parlor. They passed around baby Alta, eating tarts, mending shirts and swapping stories in an effort to keep her mind off Ben. "I remember the first time my Harry rode out," one of them said. "I was a nervous wreck, but here we are fifteen years later. I'd like to say it gets easier, but it doesn't."

The women around the little circle nodded as if to say, "Welcome to the group, you are one of us now. We worry together, we laugh together and if needed, we cry together." And Moira smiled back.

Despite the circumstances of their visit, it was a cozy evening and Moira was overwhelmed by the outpouring of support from these new friends whom she'd come to know through the school. Their husbands were home safe and yet they'd reached out to her and given of their precious time and experience. She couldn't imagine sharing this kind of time or these kinds of feelings with any of the women she'd known in New York, except perhaps Gemma. It was yet another sign of how this journey had changed her, and all she was leaving behind. She hadn't really changed, only a little perhaps, but not enough. She was still bringing trouble to those she cared about.

When conversation flagged, Maggie read to the women from a novel. After Maggie and Lizzie went to bed, Moira continued the reading well into the night until her own head began to droop and the quartermaster's wife put her to bed with the promise to wake her if there was any news.

The last thing Moira remembered was the blissfully dark oblivion of sleep rising up to meet her as her head hit the pillow. Peace at last enveloped her. Everything was going to be alright.

The ambush had gone wrong from the start and now they were likely the ones being ambushed. Ben held his pistol steady at the ready as a twig cracked in the trees beyond the rustlers' camp. He and his men stood in a circle facing outward, eyes peeled on the trees for any sign of movement. They'd tracked the rustlers to the camp and had intended to ambush it come morning, but when morning came, the place had been deserted.

After a day of lying in wait, no one had returned, which had created the need to go down and survey the camp more closely. To which, there would be one of two outcomes: One being that the camp was a ruse, that they'd been led there on purpose while the rustlers were now far away. Or, the camp was a trap. While they were watching the rustlers, the rustlers were watching them, waiting for them to blink first and go down there. Either way, Ben had given up on hopes of being home tonight or perhaps even tomorrow.

So, here they were—he and Cort in an empty camp with ten nervous young men who'd never seen any form of combat. "What was that?" The young man beside him jumped at the crack of the twig.

"Steady, Peterson," Ben said sternly, his voice low. "Might just be a squirrel." Or it might be an outlaw with a gun trained on them, Ben thought grimly. "Men, remember, we have the high ground, metaphorically speaking. We are in possession of their territory. We'll see them coming. When they do, we just stand here and pick them off, then we're homeward bound."

Unless the rustlers picked them off first, which was always a possibility. They might be in possession of the camp, but the rustlers were in possession of cover. If they were in the trees, they could choose to be snipers instead of openly confronting them. Under those conditions, Ben didn't like the odds. He'd much rather have them out in the open where he could see them, count them. Time to go to work.

Ben stepped forward slightly from the circle and raised his voice in commanding tones. "I am Major Benjamin Sheffield of the United States Army. I come with orders from the military governor in Monterey to bring in those involved in stealing government horses. Surrender yourselves now and we take you in peaceably to the fort at the Presidio where you can plead your case to a court. If not, we will take you in forcibly."

A shot rang out, whistling past Ben's ear. He fired into the trees and was rewarded with a yelp. He'd found his target. The rustlers were upon them then, rushing from cover, shooting as they came. "Fire, men! Don't let them reach the circle," Ben yelled, hearing Cort do the same. There were fifteen men bearing down on the camp. Bullets whizzed in all directions but Ben was right, they had the "high ground" and they stood it. The fight was over in less than two minutes. But what an expensive two minutes. Eight rustlers lay on the ground dead or wounded. Four were uncounted for, perhaps having slunk back into the woods. Ben's own men hadn't emerged unscathed. Two were dead and Peterson had gone down, clutching a leg and screaming.

Ben knelt beside the young man, swiftly assessing the damage. The wound was bleeding badly. He tied a bandage high and tight on the man's thigh and probed. The bullet was still in there. "We'll get you back to the fort and have the surgeon look after you. You'll be fine," he told Peterson with a confidence he didn't feel. He rose and conferred with Cort. "We need to leave immediately. There are four rustlers out there who might be regrouping." Or not. They could be licking their wounds or just hoping the soldiers would go away, but he had to prepare for the worst possible scenario.

"Why don't we split up," Cort suggested. "You head back with Peterson and I'll take the men and see if we can round up the stragglers. We'll bring the horses back, too."

Plan in place, Ben set off for the fort, leading Peterson on his horse. Ben hoped the man would make it but it was a long ride. They'd ridden most of yesterday and it was already late afternoon. He wasn't sure how he felt about traveling in the dark but he might not have a choice, not with Peterson's leg bleeding like it was.

Dark had fallen when he became aware he was being followed. Ben slowed his horse and cocked his pistol. "Peterson, look alert." Peterson had slouched in the saddle a few miles back. There wouldn't be much help from that quarter if there was trouble. Ben kept his horse moving. Every step was a step closer to home, to Moira.

The first shot took him in the arm, spooking the horses. The second shot took Peterson clean out of the saddle while Ben fought to keep his own seat. The third shot took his horse. Probably not on purpose, but a shot gone wild in the dark. Ben felt the animal go down and himself with it, his arm on fire with pain and useless. He fell hard, something sharp catching his head as he landed.

Pain rocketed through his skull, and the world swam. No, he could not lose consciousness, he scolded himself, grappling for a thread of alertness. He had to stay awake, had to fight. Somewhere beyond him was a scream. In the confusion of his brain, his instant thought was that the cry came from Moira. Was she in trouble? No, it wasn't her but his horse. He ought to do something about that, too, but he couldn't move. A new darkness encroached, one different from the night. No, he didn't want it.

He fought the darkness, holding on to thoughts of the girls, of Moira, of the life they were going to build if he could get home and make things right with her. He'd not left her on a good note. The hurt on her face when he'd gone haunted him. She thought it was her fault he'd been assigned to this mission, one more mark she made against herself right next to the marks about her cooking and inability to do laundry.

She judged herself too harshly. She was capable of so much more that mattered. She'd brought him back to life, out of his isolated cave little bit by little bit. He owed her his life in that regard. She'd brought him back to life and to love. He *loved* her. Ben winced against the pain in his shoulder. He should have told her before he left. Instead, he'd given her a pistol instead of absolution.

He should have told her he didn't blame her, that he didn't want her to change. *You've always been wild.* He regretted those harsh words. In his anger and worry, those words had been condemning. He groaned. He'd made a hash of leaving her, of creating uncertainty. Would she think he didn't want her? They'd come so far only to be undone by words spoken in a careless moment. *I'm sorry, Moira.*

Oblivion dragged him down, obliterating everything, even the pain. His mind whispered a final prayer: *Lord, be with Moira, let her know this was not her fault. She needs You.* He wasn't going to make it home to Moira, wasn't going to be able to stop her from believing the worst of herself, but perhaps the Lord would.

Chapter Twenty-Two

The men are back. The words woke Moira. The quartermaster's wife was there in her bedroom, baby on her hip, excitement in her voice. "They've been sighted coming down the road." That meant there was time to tidy herself. Moira rose quickly and splashed water on her face. She groped for a comb and ran it through the tangles of her hair. Finding it a hopeless mess, she opted to tie it back in a ribbon.

Outside, people had gathered as the bugle trumpeted the arrival and the gates opened. Only then did Moira realize it was midday. She'd slept longer than she'd thought but she felt rested and refreshed as a result and Ben was home. Her world was right again.

The first horses came through, Cort at the head looking dusty and tired but otherwise unharmed. Men were leading horses, herding them toward the corrals. That was a good sign. The mission must have been successful. It did make it hard to see everyone, though. Moira craned her neck to see around the horses, to see down the crooked column to the remaining men. Ben was probably bringing up the rear in case any horse tried to bolt.

It took a moment to realize there was no one else arriving. Moira stood frozen, trying to make sense of it all. There were horses, men, but no Ben. Was he late? Had he and a few other men stayed behind? She did see that not all of the ten men were there. "Cort!" She approached as Ben's friend dismounted. "Where's Ben?"

A question flickered across Cort's eyes before he could disguise the concern. "Is he not here? Is he not back yet?" Moira shook her head. "He had a wounded man with him," Cort explained. "He left before us. We stayed behind to round up stragglers. He should have been home early this morning."

Unless. The word hung between them. Unless something had happened. She gripped his arm. "Cort, what are you not telling me?" Fear filled her.

"We only found two of the four stragglers, Moira," he said quietly. "I hope to heaven the other two didn't find Ben."

"You would have come across him on your way back," Moira suggested, clinging to a thin sliver of hope.

"No, we came back by a different route." Decision settled in Cort's eyes. "I'm going back out." He raised his voice. "There's men still out there, men who might be hurt. I need a fresh horse!"

"I need one, too," Moira cried fiercely. She shot

Cort a silencing look when he was about to protest. "I'm going with you, Cort. Don't you dare leave without me. That's my husband out there. I need five minutes, that's all." She wasn't going to leave without seeing the girls safe and she wasn't goiing without Ben's pistol.

They rode hard. With just the two of them, they were able to travel faster than the group of ten. The hard ride kept her thoughts from running away with her but fear of the worst didn't leave her. Once again she prayed. *Lord, let him be safe.* Cort pulled up. "Moira, look." Cort pulled up, spying a downed horse on the side of that path. "That's Ben's mount." The fear gripped at her. That could not bode well for Ben. She fought it back as Cort dismounted. Cort knelt by the fallen beast. He rose, grim. "There's a bullet wound, the horse was shot." He dusted his hands on his trousers. "Stay here, I'll go scout. If this is where the horse fell, perhaps Ben is nearby."

Moira swallowed hard and jumped down. "I'm coming with you." She was not going to sit on her horse and wait, not while her husband could be at hand. Dead or alive, she was going to find him. There was a flock of crows overhead and she tried to ignore them. There'd been crows, too, on the march to the Presidio. They were generally quite populous here. It didn't have to mean anything dire, and yet she could not dismiss the fact that it was likely the dead horse that had drawn them. She hoped it was the only dead thing.

They'd only gone a short distance when Cort swore and fell to his knees. "Peterson!" Moira looked away, relief and horror battling within her. The body wasn't Ben's. She should not be glad of it. It was an unseemly reaction, and yet it meant there was still hope.

Beyond the body, a horse grazed on the sparse grass. Peterson's horse? she wondered. "Should we call for him?" Moira asked. If Ben was lying somewhere hurt, he might not be able to come to them.

"No, the rustlers might still be about." Cort stepped protectively in front of her as they continued on. Moira cocked the pistol in her pocket. If there were rustlers, she'd be ready. "Moira, we might be too late. His horse was shot," he warned.

She knew what that meant. That Ben had fallen. He was on foot, somewhere. Perhaps even now he was walking, trying to come home to her. It would be easy to get lost in the dark and they were only just now learning their way around. Or it meant that he was lying somewhere hurt or worse. She put the thought away. She couldn't think on it. *She* would break. *Please don't take him, Lord, not when I love him, not when I'm willing to leave, not when this is not his fault but mine. The girls need their father.*

"Moira, he's here!" Cort rushed forward into a little culvert up against a rock wall. "He's hit his head." Cort was on his knees beside his fallen friend, his hands in Ben's blond hair searching for injury.

"Is he alive?" Moira couldn't quite breathe. Some second sense held her rooted to the ground. They'd found Ben but in what state? He lay motionless on the ground amid the rocks, a crimson stain on the right sleeve of his coat.

"Yes, he's alive." Cort's gaze was filled with joy when he looked at her. He levered his friend into a sitting position, displacing some rocks as he did so. That's when Moira heard it, the ominous rattle of a snake's tail. The dislodged rocks had disturbed him. The snake was inches from Ben's hand!

"Cort, don't move," Moira said sternly. In a slow motion, she drew out the pistol. If she missed the snake, she'd hit Ben's hand. At this close distance, a bullet would shatter all the fine bones in that hand. But if she didn't take the shot, the Western rattler would likely sink its teeth into that hand poison and all. Cool detachment settled over Moira as she took aim. This was a shot of a lifetime. She wouldn't miss. She couldn't afford to.

She fired, the rattlesnake dropping to the ground, flaccid and lifeless. She lowered the pistol. Ben moaned and she raced to his side, kneeling beside him. "Ben, I'm here. Cort's here. You're safe." The moan was all she got. There were no fluttering eyes, no clear blue gaze meeting hers. Ben sagged in Cort's arms.

"He's been shot, and he's lost a lot of blood," Cort said. "I think he must have hit his head when he fell. I worry about jostling him home on a horse but there's nothing for it." He shook his head. "He's safe but it's no guarantee he'll make it, Moira. He's hurt badly and he's spent a night exposed to the elements, mostly unconscious." She knew what that meant. Unconscious meant he'd been without food and water. He'd be chilled and dehydrated on top of being wounded. It was a deadly combination.

"Ben, don't you dare leave me." She squeezed his hand and they began the arduous task of getting Ben home alive.

The surgeon's pronouncement after a lengthy examination was that he was lucky to be alive, his summation the same as Cort's. "He's home, my dear, but that doesn't mean he'll make it." The surgeon steered her out into the parlor. "He has a fever. It's not from infection as far as I can tell. Rather, it's from being out all night without protection. But fever is fever and it's dangerous to him nonetheless. He's dehydrated. He's got to take some water and some broth, which will be no mean feat considering he is not conscious. Truth is, I'm not sure what to be worried about the most, his head or his arm or his general condition."

"Is there no good news?" Moira snapped, more waspish than she intended. The surgeon was doing his best.

"He's not lost his arm and if the infection stays away, he'll keep it. That's good news. If the fever breaks and he can make it through the night, there's a good chance we'll get him back. I think the next twelve hours will seal his fate." The surgeon packed his bag. "Send one of the girls for me if you need me." That was his way of saying there was nothing more he could do. It was up to her now. Moira turned and went back into the bedroom.

"He's not going to die," she said fiercely to the girls and Cort, who were gathered at the bedside. "Maggie, Lizzie, fetch clean, cold water and rags to bring the fever down. One of you run to Cook and see if he has any broth, we'll need to spoon it into him." The girls were relieved to be able to do something. It had been a shock to them when Ben had been brought in.

Cort waited until the girls left before he spoke. "How bad is it?"

Moira faced him with honest eyes. "If he makes it until morning, the surgeon says there's a chance. He won't die, Cort. I won't let him." All the emotion she'd kept under control for the girls' sake welled up. "I can't lose him, Cort. He never should have been out there. It's all my fault. He deserves to be happy. He deserves a better woman like his Sarah." Her voice broke and she had to stop for fear of breaking down altogether.

"I'm so sorry, Moira. I shouldn't have had us separate. If only we'd stayed together." Cort was in anguish over his friend. He gathered himself. "If anything happens, I will make sure you and the girls are cared for, that you get back to New York. You won't be cast adrift."

"It won't be necessary, Cort," Moira said briskly. "Ben is going to live." She would save him if it was the last thing she did, and in fact it would be. Once he was safe, she'd go. "Get some rest. You can check in on him later." She saw Cort out and tied on an apron. She had work to do.

She labored through the evening, Maggie and Lizzie by her side until she sent them to bed with promises to wake them if there were any changes. She hoped she wouldn't have to. Waking them would only mean one thing. The worst had happened. For the girls it would be the second such time they'd wake to a dying parent. She hugged each of them tightly, acutely aware that this must seem like a recurring nightmare to them. "Your father is strong. He's made it this far," she encouraged them.

Then she was alone. It was up to her to save him. She was on her own and she'd never felt it more keenly than she felt it now. Not when her parents died, not even when Brandon had told her she was to marry and go to a far-off place, cut off from her family with only a stranger beside her. Ben wasn't a stranger now, but the man she loved enough to leave.

She reached for the soup bowl and tried patiently to spoon more broth into his slack mouth. "Ben, you have to eat." Some went in, some dribbled out. It seemed a losing battle but she kept at it. She changed the wet rags but that too seemed futile against the fever that warmed them soon after she laid them across his brow.

She talked to him without end. "Remember Rio? Remember the day in the market when you kissed me? I wanted you to do so much more than kiss me," she confessed. There'd been so much hope, so much potential that day. Perhaps he could hear her wherever he was. If he did, there was no sign. Unless one counted thrashing. She was desperate. She couldn't fight him, couldn't do this alone. What would Ben say? What would Ben do?

He would pray. The answer came to her swift and sure. Ben was never alone. Ben was certain that God was with him always, even in darkness. Ben had prayed for the storm to abate, Ben had prayed for Lizzie to get well. Even when Lizzie had nearly slipped away from them, Ben had prayed. He'd never given up the belief that he was not alone. Not like her. Moira had felt alone since she was ten and she'd lost everything in her little world. Now she stood poised to lose it all again. God could not be that cruel. Ben would want her to pray. Ben would want her to know she wasn't alone.

So for the first time in over a decade, Moira prayed as if the prayer would be answered, prayed as if there was no doubt lurking in the back of her mind that this was a pro forma act only, but an act of real belief.

She must have prayed until she'd fallen asleep, her head on the bed beside Ben, her hand clasped in his good one. When she awoke somewhere near dawn, she thought she heard voices singing. Perhaps it was some lingering remnant of a dream. But the more awake she became, the more prominent the singing. She'd not imagined it.

Maggie padded in barefoot, a quilt wrapped around her shoulders. "Mama Moira, come and see, just for a moment. The regiment is here."

It was hard for Moira to leave Ben for even a minute for fear he would choose that moment to slip away from her, but Maggie stayed behind so that Ben wasn't alone. Through the windows of the parlor, Moira could see the lanterns and candles flicker in the hands of their holders, casting light on the faces she'd come to know so well in the past eight months. The regiment was there, Cort was there, the quartermaster and his wife were there, Cook was there and others as well. New friends. She recognized the faces of some of the Mormon mothers who brought their children to the "fort school." They'd come down from the hills. What a walk that must have been and in the dark, too. All to keep a candlelight vigil for Ben. For her.

Moira went out to them to thank them, tears in her eyes. "I wish I had breakfast to give you all. Ben will be so touched you did this for him."

The quartermaster's wife took her hand. "And for you. You are not alone, Moira. Your fight is our fight. We are all in this together." For her. They were here for her. *She wasn't alone.* She did cry then. God had heard one prayer. Had he heard the other? Perhaps he might have and it gave her hope. Beyond them, the sun began to come up over the bay. An Easter verse came unbidden to her mind. *On the third day he rose again from dead.* Morning had broken and Ben was still alive.

She went back inside to relieve Maggie and knelt beside the bed, gripping Ben's hand, gratitude on her lips. *Thank You, God. Thank You, thank You.* Then she felt it, the faintest of pressures against her hand, the slightest of squeezes. Ben was coming home. To her. So she could say goodbye.

Chapter Twenty-Three

They were singing him home, drawing him back from heat and darkness. He was burning, or he had been burning. It was better now. His body had been a cauldron of temperatures, his mind a muddle of memories.

No matter how hard he tried he couldn't sort through the images, couldn't make any order out of them. He'd been shot. There'd been pain in his arm, in his head. There'd been blood and darkness and more pain. His horse was dead. He was lost in the wilderness, unable to move. He remembered freezing and wishing for warmth, then warmth had come and never left.

How was he to get home if he couldn't move? Then he'd heard Moira's voice and knew he must be delirious. How could she be in the wilderness? She was at home with the girls. There was a bang like the report of pistol. He'd given Moira a pistol before he'd left. She was the best shot in Manhattan.

He was back at the house party now at Mrs. Bostwick's. Moira was on the back lawn tossing her head and challenging Eddie Brant. He couldn't stop watching her, couldn't stop wondering what she'd do next. This was definitely dreams, this had already happened. He had to rouse himself but he simply couldn't. He was thirsty and hot and his strength had failed completely.

I don't want to die. The girls need me. Moira loves me. There's so much to explore with her yet, a whole life to live. There's her forgiveness to beg for leaving her as I did. But what he wanted seemed so far beyond him. He couldn't recall ever being this helpless. He couldn't even fight for himself. But someone was fighting for him. Someone was shoving warm broth down his throat. Someone was putting out the fire of his fever with cold, soothing rags. He knew that touch.

Moira. She was here with him even at the last. She was praying. It must be very nearly over, then, if she'd resorted to that, his beautiful Moira, who thought God ignored her. She was praying for him. He couldn't let her be disappointed this time. Somewhere in his fevered mind a prayer came to him. *Please don't let her down, Lord. She needs to know You're there. Answer her prayer.* And he began to fight. For Moira and the very depths of her not-quite-believing soul. He gathered his strength and squeezed her hand.

He squeezed his right hand around a ball of soft fabric, feeling it give beneath the pressure of his fingers. The surgeon smiled. "Progress indeed, Major Sheffield. I think we can safely say there will be no damage to your arm. You're recovering nicely."

"I'm recovering *slowly*," Ben groused. It had been nearly a week and he was still confined to bed, still felt pathetically weak after sitting up for only a few hours. Moira had let him sit in the parlor yesterday to visit with Cort and he'd fallen asleep after a half an hour.

"You had a very close call, Major. Recovery at any speed is to be appreciated and you are doing exceptionally well," the surgeon scolded kindly. "I'll tell your wife you can add a bit of meat to your diet starting tonight. That should be cause for celebration."

It was indeed one cause for celebration but there was still a cause for worry. His body might be out of danger but his marriage was not. The stronger he became, the more Moira withdrew. There'd been no chance to tell her what was in his heart. "Send my wife in when you leave," Ben asked. It was time to heal the last of the wounds.

"I hear you are to have meat." Moira came in with a stack of fresh laundry and a smile that didn't hide the sadness in her eyes.

"Come sit beside me." He patted the space on the bed, the little gesture thrilling him beyond measure. He'd nearly lost his arm, his life. "We must talk. I have things to say."

Moira sat and shook her head. "You needn't say anything. I'll leave. There's a ship next week to New York. You can tell the girls whatever you like. You can tell people you cast me off. I'll take all the blame so that no one will judge you."

Ben was silent, his gaze steady on his beautiful, proud wife. She truly had no idea how good her heart was. "Absolutely not, Moira. You are my wife and I have no intention of being apart from you. What I want to tell people is what I should have told you a long time ago. I love you."

"You shouldn't love me. You nearly died because of me. You're right, I'm wild, I haven't changed."

He gripped her hand with his good one for fear she'd move away from him. "What happened was not your fault. If anyone is to blame, it's Shelby for not being able to conduct himself as a gentleman should. It's not a sin to speak your mind." He sighed and fell back against the pillows. "When I lay on the ground, thinking I was going to die, my only thoughts were for you and they were ones of regret—regret that I'd left as I did, leaving you room to doubt yourself and doubt me, and regret that I hadn't told you I loved you."

He loved her. It was an embarrassment of riches, really, to hear those words, to see that love in his eyes, and she couldn't stop the tears. He didn't want her to leave. He didn't blame her. "I don't deserve you, Ben. I'll only mess things up." She had to warn him, protect him.

"You can't mess up love, Moira." He squeezed her hand. "*You* shot a rattlesnake for me, Moira. I think that's my new favorite story. I'm sorry to have missed actually seeing you shoot the rattlesnake, but Cort tells it so well it's almost worth it." Moira blushed. Cort's telling of the story got better and the snake got bigger every time he told it. It was becoming quite the tall tale.

Ben sobered and a soft look passed between them. "You've done more than shoot the snake that almost took off my good hand. You sailed nearly halfway around the world for me. You've given me my family back, my life back. It's a good thing we aren't keeping score because I would be in your debt forever."

"And you have given me back my faith," Moira offered quietly. He made it seem as if he'd done nothing for her. "You do not come to me empty-handed. You've given me a place in the world, a sense of fulfillment that only comes from being by your side."

"So, no more talk of leaving to save me from myself? I would be lost without you, Moira. There is nothing I want more than to live this adventure with my bold, sometimes outrageous wife by my side, always, starting today, now that I can hold a pen. Do you know what that means? It means we can start our store and our school in town.

"This last mission has reminded me how precious life is and how insecure. There are no guarantees. I want to enjoy every moment with you and my girls. I want to spend it doing good work and I can no longer do that work in the military. Would you send word to Colonel Stevenson that I'd like to speak with him right away?"

"Resign? Are you sure? The military has been

your life," Moira cautioned him. "You don't have to do this for me or because of Shelby." Shelby had been released from the jail and demoted from his position, which had not subdued his temper.

"I am doing this for *us*. You are my life now. You and the girls. I have given this much thought and prayer just as you asked me to." Love sparked unmistakably in his eyes. "I am sure this is the path for our family."

Hope flooded her. Happiness swamped her. It had not been taken, after all. It was still there, still alive amid the worry and turmoil of the last weeks. Ben loved her. Ben wanted a life, a family with her, and the knowledge of that filled her with a completeness that surpassed anything she knew.

She was home, not because she was in San Francisco, but because she was loved by this man. Home would be wherever they were together. He levered up from his pillow to kiss her gently on the lips.

"Ben, there's something I should I tell you first." She leaned her forehead against his.

"What? Have you expanded the enrollment at your school again?" He laughed.

"No, it's nothing like that. It's much more serious," she teased, enjoying keeping him on his proverbial toes. "I love you."

"That's all?" Ben's eyes twinkled, teasing in return.

"That's all? Why, I should think that is quite enough." Moira smiled.

"It is, Moira. More than enough. More than you'll ever know." But she did know because he loved her, too. The future was theirs to shape as they liked, together, all because they'd allowed themselves to be transformed by love.

Chapter Twenty-Four

San Francisco, June 1852
Sheffield's Department Store and Greengrocer

Moira jiggled the toddler on her hip behind the store counter as she helped two women with their purchases. Joshua was two and a half and had the patience one might expect of someone that age, especially when it came to boring affairs like the grand reopening of his papa's department store. The ribbon had been cut just this morning and business was brisk as a result.

"Let me take him." Her sister in-law, Gemma, came to the rescue. "When you're finished here, come sit down. You've been on your feet all day and you've got to think about your condition." That condition being six months pregnant with a brother or sister for Joshua and the girls at the beginning of autumn. That impending birth had been one of the major impetuses for Gemma and Brandon's visit. The fire in San Francisco eleven months ago had been the other.

Gemma spirited Joshua away and Moira turned back to the customers. It felt good to be busy. This year had been harder than the others. When the fire had torn through San Francisco and destroyed the city, over a thousand homes had been lost and businesses, too, including their first store. But they rebuilt, thanks to help from family. Gemma and Brandon had arrived with Ethan aboard one of Brandon's ships. The ship had been loaded with merchandise for the store to replace what had been lost in the fire and Brandon had been keen to see how the gold rush had transformed San Francisco and to assess business opportunities.

It had been the work of this past year to restock to the level they'd been at before the fire of 1851. It wasn't the first fire. Fire seemed to be a regular villain to town. There'd been seven in the last four years but the last one had been the worst. Still, they'd persevered, supported by their love for one another even in the face of adversity. They had built back, bigger and grander than before, and this was the result.

This store was a real department store, two stories tall and taking up a full city block. It was filled with everything imaginable: furniture from the East Coast, fabric, silk from the Orient, mining supplies, including canvas pants for men headed to the goldfields. Just a few months ago, Ben had struck up a deal with a Bavarian named Strauss looking for places to sell his durable clothing.

Today, canvas pants were flying off the shelves. There were toys and candy and hair bows, at Lizzie's request. Whatever anyone wanted, one could find it at Sheffield's Department Store. That had been the case before the fire and it was doubly the case now. They were insured now, too. If a fire were to happen again, they'd be protected.

Maggie came in from the school across the street ready to relieve her. "Mama, you really must rest." At seventeen, Maggie was a whirlwind of efficiency. She taught lessons in the morning at the school, also rebuilt from the fire, also another dream lost and reestablished. The Sheffields had not been daunted by flames.

"Thank you, Maggie." Moira hugged the girl, who was as tall as she was these days and a stunning beauty. Moira was going to miss her when Maggie went back to New York with Gemma and Brandon but there were opportunities there for her, socially and educationally. Maggie was determined to attend college and had her sights set on Mount Holyoke with the intention of returning to San Francisco to teach. Lizzie was more interested in the store than school these days, but that was fine with Moira. She liked that Lizzie was finding her own interests.

Moira finished with her customers and turned the counter over to Maggie. She headed to the back room, where Gemma entertained Joshua and his cousin,

Ethan. If the year had been one of hard work building back from tragedy, there had also been joy, too.

Gemma smiled as Moira entered. "Gold's been good to you. Fire notwithstanding, you and Ben have done well. You nearly rival Stewart's."

Moira laughed and picked up her son. "Nearly. I doubt we'll ever be a shopping retreat for ladies." The elegance of Stewart's seemed a lifetime ago. San Francisco was still too rough for such genteel luxury. "But we have come a long ways."

They'd started small, in 1847, before gold had been discovered. They'd lived over the store Benjamin founded, choosing to put their efforts into the business instead of splitting their funds between the business and a house for the first years. Ben had worked hard to develop relationships with local farmers using his uncle's business model. The greengrocery part of the store had been an especial success. Ben had the store, but he'd also had a wagon he drove around, selling produce out of the back end to those who couldn't get to town.

Then gold had hit and San Francisco had boomed. There hadn't been enough room in the store to carry everything they could sell. So, they'd expanded and it had been a solid success ever since.

"Ben has a knack, perhaps from his uncle or from his military experience, for knowing what men need to go adventuring and the store carried it all," Moira said. Even after the gold rush, which would end at some point, the store would continue to thrive. San Francisco was established now, California an official state. Last year alone, so many ships had arrived in the bay they had to wait days before having a place to dock.

Gemma gave a wry smile. "Ben isn't the only one with a knack for the business. This is your store, too. The women like to do business with you. You're good with them. They feel more comfortable with you, even the Spanish women and the Indians."

Moira blushed at Gemma's compliment and set Joshua down to play on the floor. "I think peace is made in such ways, through women and trade. Leave it to us and there might never be another war," She laughed, but she meant it. She liked learning about other cultures and she liked spending time with the women who came to the store to trade with her and to sell things. She liked being able to carry their goods in the store, to know that ships carried those goods back to the East Coast and that those markets provided these women with a modest income, money they made on their own, money they weren't reliant on a man for.

"Are you happy, Moira?" Gemma asked softly. "You have a good life here, one you have worked hard for and built from the ground up"

Moira looked at her son playing, and covered her belly with her hand. "So happy, Gemma. I have three children and one on the way, an adoring husband and a place in a thriving community that I am helping to build."

She and Ben were committed to supporting churches and schools in San Francisco as a means of counterbalancing the wildness that had blown into the city with the gold rush. "These are dreams I could not have imagined for myself." Dreams she hadn't even known she had. But that was the beauty of turning one's life entirely over to God. The journey was ongoing and she didn't have to be in charge, she didn't have to make the journey alone. She had Benjamin, her family and her faith whatever came: fire, earthquakes, economic depression.

The door to the back room opened, nearly slamming against its hinges as Ben and Brandon raced in, spilling with excitement. "There's gold!" Brandon announced.

"More gold? Where is it this time?" Gemma asked, patient with her husband.

"Australia!" Brandon waved a newspaper. "They've found gold in Australia."

"Do you know what that means?" Benjamin was equally as excited. "It means those canvas pants prices are going to go sky-high. Ships will put in at San Francisco before heading to Australia. This will be their last point of supply. Between both gold rushes, we won't be able to keep the shelves stocked."

"It means we'll have a new market to ship to," Brandon said and she could see her brother's mind was racing. "Americans who go to Australia are likely to stay in Australia. They'll want American goods."

Gemma and Moira laughed at their husbands. Moira rose and took Ben's hand. She slanted Benjamin a knowing look, her other hand on her belly. "Just remember, the real gold is right here."

In family, in friends, in faith. Those were the things that brought contentment. She'd learned at last those were the firmest foundations.

* * * * *

Dear Reader,

This is my first book for Love Inspired Historical, and I'm so glad to share Moira and Ben's journey—geographically, spiritually, and emotionally—with you. I hope you enjoy the settings for this story—1840s New York, the USS *Loo Choo* and pre-gold rush San Francisco.

In the 1840s, department stores were still a new idea in U.S. cities. The visit to Stewart's is as authentic as I could make it. Stewart's was New York's first department store. There are good primary records of Stevenson's regiment's journey and I tried to be as true to those records as possible. The baptism in Rio de Janeiro of Alta California really happened. Men washed overboard in the Cape Horn storm happened as well. The officers' ball really did take place at the Presidio in May. I have highlighted these events and others on my Facebook page.

Blessings,
Elizabeth Rowan

LOVE INSPIRED

Stories to uplift and inspire

Fall in love with Love Inspired—
inspirational and uplifting stories of faith
and hope. Find strength and comfort in
the bonds of friendship and community.
Revel in the warmth of possibility and the
promise of new beginnings.

Sign up for the Love Inspired newsletter
at **LoveInspired.com** to be the first
to find out about upcoming titles,
special promotions and exclusive content.

CONNECT WITH US AT:

 Facebook.com/LoveInspiredBooks

Twitter.com/LoveInspiredBks

Get 4 FREE REWARDS!

We'll send you 2 FREE Books plus 2 FREE Mystery Gifts.

FREE
Value Over
$20

Both the **Love Inspired**® and **Love Inspired**® Suspense series feature compelling novels filled with inspirational romance, faith, forgiveness, and hope.

IF YOU ENJOYED THIS BOOK
WE THINK YOU WILL ALSO LOVE

LOVE INSPIRED

INSPIRATIONAL ROMANCE

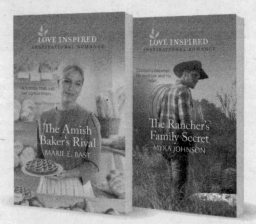

Uplifting stories of faith, forgiveness and hope.

Fall in love with stories where faith helps
guide you through life's challenges, and discover
the promise of a new beginning.

6 NEW BOOKS AVAILABLE EVERY MONTH!

LIXSERIES2021